Dear Reader,

When the I PROMISE School opened its doors in 2018 in my hometown of Akron, Ohio, it was one of the best days of my life. I will never forget walking those halls, feeling the excitement in every single classroom and seeing kids smiling from ear to ear, so happy just to be at school. It is easily one of my proudest achievements, and something I will continue my commitment to forever.

Since even before I entered the NBA, I've always wanted to give back to my community and create positive change in any way I can. I want to inspire and empower the youth and their families by offering them the kinds of educational and everyday supports I wish I'd had access to when I was growing up. Because I know these kids. I know their lives and challenges. I was them not all that long ago. Being blessed with the platform I have, I feel a responsibility to do everything I can to give them a fighting chance to realize their dreams and achieve everything I know they're capable of.

Through this story, I hope you and everyone who reads it knows that nothing is impossible if you put your mind to it.

We Are Family.

—LeBron James

WE ARE FAMILY

WE ARE FAMILY

BY

LeBron James

AND **ANDREA WILLIAMS**

HARPER
An Imprint of HarperCollins Publishers

First Edition

To my wife, Savannah; Bronny; Bryce; and Zhuri, and
to my mother, Gloria, everything I do is for you.
—LeBron James

To all in search of family, and hope:
may you find it in abundance.
—Andrea Williams

CHAPTER 1

JAYDEN CARR IS RESTLESS. He's always restless, always anxious and stirring, always unsettled in body and mind. It has been this way all his life, or at least as long as he can remember. But today? Today is different. Today is Jayden's first day of seventh grade at Carter Middle School, and for Jayden—a kid with D-I dreams, NBA fantasies, and a silky-smooth jumper he prays will get him there—the first day of school can mean only one thing.

Hoop Group

It is 4:57, not even five a.m., but Jayden is wide awake, unable to sleep but pretending to, careful not to let Grams know that he's up before the sun once again. He lies perfectly still. Even a slight shift on the saggy twin-sized mattress that's been pushed into the smallest room of his grandma's two-bedroom house could wake her. The walls are too thin, the bed too old, and the softest creak or groan would send Grams right into Jayden's room. She would stand over him then, hands on hips, tongue tsk-tsking behind tight lips. And then she would fuss. She would chastise Jayden for going back on his word, but she would do it in a sort of whisper-yell, careful not to wake his mother sleeping up front on the living room couch.

Jayden closes his eyes tight, squeezes them so hard it feels like his head might explode. More than trying to fall back asleep, he wants to empty his mind of the guilt that greets him every morning. No matter the strength of the mental fortresses he erects, how high the walls may stand around the perimeter of his thoughts, the shame of sleeping in a bed when his mother cannot sneaks in like particles of dust. They are invisible until they're not. They are harmless until they're not, until they come in with such force that it becomes hard to breathe.

Jayden is only twelve, but he is smart enough to know that it isn't *really* his fault that his mom has to fold her legs onto Grams's tiny love seat each night, making herself into a human pretzel just to sleep. The problem is,

Jayden's not really sure who *is* at fault.

Jayden's mom found out she was pregnant right before his dad was supposed to leave on his first tour of duty, but she never told him. She didn't want her boyfriend to worry about his unborn child while trying to keep himself alive in some foreign land, so she decided to carry the weight of the pregnancy alone. She quietly dropped out of law school to take care of Jayden and figured she'd tell Jevon he was going to be a father when he got back to Ohio—once he was home again, safe again.

Jayden was only three when Jevon returned to their tiny apartment. He was too young to remember how his father's face crumpled into confusion, then outrage, when he came face-to-face with the toddler who looked oddly like him. Jayden doesn't remember the yelling and the crying, either. He doesn't remember how angry his dad was that his mom had kept such a big secret, or how angry his mom was that his dad could be anything but thrilled to find out that he had a son.

It wasn't until Jayden was in the second grade that his mom finally told him what happened, that Jevon had disappeared the very next day after meeting his son for the first time.

Jayden was still a baby then, but now he understands that that's when everything started to fall apart. And now that he's older, he knows that he can't blame everything on his dad, no matter how much Grams and his mom try to. His dad might have left, but he wasn't responsible for the whole town changing and leaving so many families in a bind. It wasn't Jevon's fault that all but one of Lorain's plastic plants closed, that all those health and beauty companies opted to get their spray bottles and lotion pumps on the cheap overseas. Jayden remembers the day Greymont, the last factory standing, finally closed its own doors. He remembers how all those hardworking men and women—friends and neighbors and even his own mother, who was working at Greymont as a corporate paralegal—were suddenly out of jobs.

Once Greymont closed, hardship settled over the city like a December fog. Like so many other families, Jayden and his mom had to learn to make do with a lot less. For them, that meant making themselves at home with Grams, moving into a neighborhood that was long past its best days. They were grateful to have that option, honestly, and soon, Grams's house became Jayden's home. It was the only one he'd ever really known.

Jayden is still staring at the ceiling above his bed when, finally, he hears it: Grams is rustling in the kitchen, making her first cup of coffee for the day. He smiles. Like the buzzer at tip-off, the sound is the permission he has been waiting for, and, within minutes, he is dressed in shorts and a T-shirt. After a quick dip in the bathroom to brush his teeth and wash his face, Jayden is standing at the entrance to the kitchen, basketball in hand.

"That sure was fast," Grams says, without ever turning away from the coffeepot on the kitchen counter. "You make sure you got all the sleep outta your eyes?"

"Yes, ma'am," Jayden says, even as he instinctively wipes the corners of his eyes, just to be sure. He never understood how Grams could see without seeing, how she always knew where Jayden was and what he was doing. They say moms have eyes in the backs of their heads, but grandmas must have an extra set of eyes completely detached from their bodies, floating through space and hovering above their grandchildren's heads like the thought bubbles you see in comic books.

Jayden watches as Grams heaps two spoonfuls of sugar

into her mug and waits for the green light. "Okay, but don't be out too long, now. Get your shots in and get on back so you can get ready for school."

"Yes, ma'am."

Jayden crosses the small kitchen and gives Grams a quick kiss on the cheek. He then tiptoes through the adjoining living room, passes his mother still sleeping on the couch, and quietly heads out the front door.

It's their everyday routine, this conversation between Grams and Jayden. Grams knows how much Jayden loves to play basketball, how he sees it as his ticket out of Lorain and the 1,400-square-foot bungalow on the corner of Marsh and Seventeenth Street. During his waking hours, after the shame of darkness has passed, any guilt that Jayden carries about his family's circumstances is replaced by responsibility—a responsibility that he believes he can best fulfill on the basketball court.

So at the beginning of sixth grade, Jayden and Grams made a deal: Grams would keep an eye out in the early mornings so Jayden could hit the Blocks while his mother slept, but only if Jayden took care of his other obligations first. He had to have all his homework done the night before, no scrambling to finish math problems or science lessons at the breakfast table. And he would have to get up early, really early. Basketball was fine—good, even—but it was not to get in the way of Jayden's studies or the rest of the household. Grams made that super clear.

The agreement was easy enough for Jayden, since he never slept much anyway. How could he when his mom never really did? How could he rest knowing that her job working crazy hours for the lawyer with the neon-colored billboard along Route 70—We Don't Get Paid Unless YOU DO!—barely paid enough to make ends meet? He couldn't, really, so every morning Jayden got up when Grams did, always by 5:30 but often even earlier. And every morning he walked down to the Blocks, the neighborhood court where legends were built and cowards were broken.

Each day Jayden's workout was the same: fifty layups from the left and fifty from the right, a hundred free throws, a hundred jump shots. There is a method to this madness, of course. Jayden is a two guard, a solid catch-and-shooter who can penetrate if he needs to but prefers to pull up and drain the mid-range bucket. For this reason, he works his shot, over and over again, until muscle memory kicks in and he can make the net swish with his eyes closed.

Over the summer, Jayden began to finally see the fruits of his labor when he started spending both mornings and afternoons hooping at the Blocks. Mom was busy working, which left Grams in charge, but as long as Jayden was home by dark, Grams didn't care how many hours he spent on the court. Come nightfall, everyone knows that the Blocks get sketchy. But at midday, especially when the sun is cooking, the Blocks are about the safest place in the world. No one but the most dedicated of ballers are out then, and those are the guys Jayden loves to play against.

A lot of the guys Jayden went up against were high schoolers, sixteen- and seventeen-year-olds rocking full mustaches and size-14 shoes. Still, Jayden showed up every day—sneaks laced, muscles stretched, and, most of the time, holding his own. He was smaller (and slower) than the other guys, so he couldn't speed past them, couldn't shoot over them in man-to-man. But in a zone, if he could swivel around a defender and get free, all he needed was a moment. He knew his shot was money, that he only needed enough time for the pads of his fingers to graze the rock before he let it fly. And in those moments, when the net *popped* as the basketball whipped through and the crowd *ooh*ed and *aah*ed over the little kid with the big game, Jayden also knew that those before-dawn workouts had been worth it.

As Jayden takes his first couple of dribbles on the morning of the first day of seventh grade, his chest swells with pride at the memory of his ability to hang with some of the guys from Carter High's varsity team. It's not long, though, before that familiar anxiety takes over, before the imaginary opposition appears on the court, arms outstretched, knees bent, ready to stop Jayden mid-stride.

Instantly, Jayden's game turns on. He drives into the lane with his right hand. Then he crosses to his left, sinking a hook shot just as magical as any of the ones Magic ever hit. Next, he dribbles around the perimeter, imagines a defender with a hand in his face, and leaps off both feet to hit a long two at the top of the key.

Jayden can feel the sweat starting to gather on his forehead and across the bridge of his nose, but there is no stopping him, especially not now, not this year. Hoop Group is the best youth basketball program in the state, the same program that gave Lorain's own Kendrick King—Mr. Triple Double—his start. Jayden's game is nothing like Kendrick's, but he has big respect for him. He also knows that if Kendrick King can go from Hoop

Group all the way to the League, Jayden can, too.

Winded, Jayden bends forward, pulling the hem of his shorts taut over his kneecaps and drawing in two long, deep breaths. On his third, as Jayden tries to slow the racing thoughts in his mind, the air catches in his throat and his heartbeat starts to pick up speed. Jayden had thought he was the only one on the court, but now, as he gets a glimpse of the far baseline in his periphery, he realizes that he wasn't alone after all.

Someone has been standing by, watching.

CHAPTER 2

JAYDEN IS STILL CATCHING HIS BREATH when the stranger starts walking toward him. With each step the man grows bigger and bigger, his massive frame blocking the just-rising sun.

"What's good, li'l homey?" the man says once he is close enough to extend his hand to Jayden in a casual greeting.

With the man now directly in front of him, Jayden is still struck by the size of the him—he must be at least 6'8", 275—but Jayden is no longer nervous about his strangeness. Deep, soft creases form around the man's eyes when he smiles, making him seem nice. Friendly, even. Jayden extends his own hand, and they dap, reaching muscled arms behind the other's back in that universal embrace of Black men old and not so old.

"I've been checking you out," the man continues. "You got skills. How long you been hooping?"

Jayden's breathing and heart rate have finally slowed to comfortable. He smiles at the compliment. "I started playing seriously when I was seven, so like five years."

The man nods, stroking his goateed chin, and Jayden senses something familiar about him, like maybe he isn't a stranger after all. "I can tell you been putting in work," the man says. "But you don't always come out this early, do you?"

"Well, during the school year I do." Jayden picks up the ball, crouches low, and starts passing it back and forth between his hands before moving it between his legs in an effortless figure eight. "I hooped down here during the summer, but mostly in the afternoons."

"Ah, gotcha. That explains it, then. I started coming out in June to get some shots in—nothing serious—but I always come early when I can have the court to myself. I thought I woulda noticed you before."

"Oh, you ball?" Jayden asks.

"Nah. Not for real. Used to, though. Now I'm just

trying to stay in shape." The man chuckles, pats a mid-section that's not exactly firm but is far from fat. Then he stops short, as if suddenly remembering that he'd left the oven on, or the garage door up. "My bad, dude. I'm Roddy. Roddy Buckner. I grew up around here and used to play at Willow Brook back in the day."

Jayden nods, returns the introduction, and, all at once, remembers. He doesn't know Roddy, but he knows *of* him. Everybody in Lorain does. Roddy played high school ball with Kendrick, and, together, they were considered the best inside-out prep duo in the country. Mr. Triple Double probably would have been Mr. Double Double if he didn't have Roddy to dish to. Meanwhile, Roddy earned the nickname Buckets because he just hung out beneath the basket, banking every pass or offensive rebound that came his way, too big and too dominant for anyone to stop him. He graduated from Willow Brook Academy the same year as Kendrick and was a lock for Kentucky or Kansas, or even to follow in MJ's footsteps at North Carolina. But then, just as it was taking off, his career was suddenly over.

"So tell me," Roddy says, interrupting Jayden's thoughts, "what makes you wanna get up so early to work when all the other kids your age are probably still turning over in their beds?"

Jayden shifts from the figure eights to a dribbling drill. *One-two-three* dribbles on the left, *one-two-three* dribbles on the right, *one-two-three* . . . "I'm getting ready for Hoop Group," he says, his brows knitted in concentration. "I played last year, but I'm in seventh grade this year, and—"

"This is the year that counts," Roddy says, finishing his sentence.

Jayden nods. He doesn't have to mention that seventh grade is the year when the people who matter start paying attention, when kids start getting scouted by local private schools and the best ones are offered scholarships for eighth grade. For those kids, eighth-grade ball leads to one of the top high school teams in the area, to the teams that provide the training and the platform necessary to play Division I basketball and, eventually, go pro. Most important for Jayden, landing a spot on one of those teams will be the first step to ensuring that his mom never has to sleep on the couch again. No matter what may have happened to Lorain when all the jobs left, basketball was still a way out. And for kids like Jayden, it all starts with Hoop Group.

"Well," Roddy says, stealing the ball from Jayden with one quick swipe, "if you're down, I can show you a couple of things."

Jayden's face goes bright like the July sun on a cloudless day. "Yeah! That would be dope!"

"Cool." Roddy tosses the ball back to Jayden. "Let me see you drive to the basket."

As Jayden dribbles back out, just beyond the three-point line, a calm washes over him. His arms and legs are loose, his eyes steady, his mind steeled. He considers doing a spin move—something he thinks will surely impress Roddy—but he changes his mind. He chooses the efficient over the extravagant and decides to cross from his right to his left hand, ending with a reverse layup.

Jayden goes out wide and picks up speed as he starts his drive. He's coasting, pushing, just a few steps outside the lane. Then, at the last minute, he looks up to see Roddy slide into the paint, his wide shoulders forming an impenetrable wall just in front of the basket. Without hesitating, Jayden picks ups his dribble and stops in his tracks.

"What are you doing?" Roddy says.

"I—I was driving. I was doing what you said, but then I saw you . . . I saw you, and—"

"And what?"

"And I didn't know you were gonna guard me."

"So you're saying you can't drive if somebody's guarding you?"

Jayden sighs, shifts his weight from his right leg to his left. "No. I didn't say that. I just wasn't expecting you to step in front of me like that. And you're . . . big. Way bigger than me. Nobody I play against is gonna be that big."

"Okay. Help me understand, then." Roddy grabs the bill of his cap and slides it around to the back, freeing his face of the shadows that had been crisscrossing his deep brown skin. "I see somebody getting up when it's still dark outside, putting in work while everybody else sleeps, and I assume he's trying to ride this thing till the wheels fall off. Play D-I, make millions in the NBA, take care of his family." He pauses, lets his expression go hard. "But maybe I got it all wrong."

Jayden waits for Roddy to say something else, to ask a question, perhaps, but he says nothing. He only waits.

"That *is* what I want," Jayden says finally. "I wanna make it to the League, and I wanna take care of my mom and my grandma. I wanna make it so my mom never has to work again. I mean, she'll probably work anyway just 'cause I think she likes to stay busy, but I want her to work for fun. Not 'cause she has to." Jayden stops talking then and lets his eyelids drop. He can feel it coming again, the stabbing sense that he's not doing enough for the woman who's done everything for him.

"Okay," Roddy says. "That's exactly what I thought. But let me ask you this: Do you think it's gonna be easy to make all that happen?"

Jayden smirks and tries to hide his embarrassment. "Nah. I mean, of *course* it won't be easy. I got a cousin that played at Wake Forest. We're not close or anything, but I know how hard he had to go to play in the ACC. He was hitting the weight room first thing in the morning, then conditioning in the afternoon, going to practice, watching film—"

Roddy holds up a giant hand to cut off Jayden's words, and the hand is all Jayden can see, as if the moon has eclipsed the sun. "That ain't what I'm talkin 'bout. The gym? The weight room? That's the easy part. It's everything else in your life that's gonna be hard."

"I don't know what you mean," Jayden says.

Once again, Roddy takes the ball from Jayden's hands. "This right here?" he says, holding the brown orb high.

"You got this. It's in you. You're a baller, and balling comes easy. But being able to hoop ain't enough to get you to college or the League. Trust me on that."

"What does it take, then?"

"The main thing," Roddy says, "is that you gotta know how to see a challenge and keep driving to the goal anyway."

There is a minute of silence before Jayden says quietly, "Like when you stepped into the lane, right? I stopped when I should have kept going and tried to score."

"Exactly," Roddy says. "All you knew was that I was bigger and stronger than you. But you didn't know what woulda happened if you woulda actually went up against me. I coulda defended you close and forced a miss, or I coulda blocked your shot completely. But on the flip side, you coulda driven in, shot around me, and scored anyway. Or, most likely—and especially if I was a kid your age—I woulda fouled you and you'da been on the line."

Roddy fires the ball back at Jayden, who catches it at his chest. "The point is that you can't stop. No matter how big the dude in the paint is."

Jayden nods, and with fire in his belly, he dribbles back outside the arc. "I'm ready now," he says. "Watch."

"I wish I could, li'l man," Roddy says, glancing at his phone, "but I got a feeling you probably need to get ready for school."

In an instant, Jayden's stomach clenches tight like Grams's teeth when she catches Jayden playing *NBA 2K* instead of studying. He'd completely forgotten about the time. Now Grams is going to kill him, and what a slow, torturous death it will be. He can hear her now: *You're a student-athlete, not an athlete-student, Jayden. Don't you ever get it twisted.*

With his mouth dry like sandpaper and nervous perspiration dotting his hairline, Jayden quickly thanks Roddy for talking to him and waves goodbye.

At that point, there is only one thing left to do: *RUN.*

CHAPTER 3

JAYDEN IS A LIVING, BREATHING MIRACLE—and not just because he made it to school on time (courtesy of a three-and-a-half-minute shower), or because Grams didn't smite him before he could become a real-life teenager. (*The good Lord has bestowed me with a little extra grace this morning, just for you*, she'd said.)

No. Jayden is a miracle because it is 1:52 p.m., right before the last period of the day, and he has managed to walk nearly every hallway of Carter Middle, plus the library and cafeteria, all while keeping his brand-new Kendrick Kings just as crisp and unscuffed as they were when he pulled them out of the box that morning.

Indeed, if meeting Roddy Buckner was a big "welcome to seventh grade and the rest of your life" chocolate cake with three layers and a crunchy cookie middle, scoring the latest KKs was a mound of whipped buttercream icing, light and fluffy and drizzled with a strawberry glaze that spelled Jayden's name in swoopy cursive.

Jayden was surprised to find that his mom had already left for work by the time he got back from the Blocks. Her boss wanted her there an hour earlier than normal, so she couldn't kiss Jayden goodbye on his first day of school like she normally did. Jayden wasn't upset or sad about it, though, because once Grams told him that his mom had left something special for him on his bed, anticipation shoved any negative feelings aside.

Grams made Jayden jump in the shower before he even thought about checking out his gift—*Do* not *pass go, and do not collect $200,* she'd said—but 210 seconds later, he was standing, dripping wet and jaw slack, in front of the most wonderful surprise he'd ever gotten.

Jayden dressed quickly in his solid polo and khaki shorts, loosened the strings on his new kicks so that he could get his foot in with ease—sans creasing—and slipped them on ever so carefully. Then he stood up and angled his foot right and left, as if he was the newest kid endorser for Kendrick King Sneakers and Apparel, posing for his very own advertisement.

His heart was as full as his stomach on Thanksgiving night, but there was something else, too. It was that feeling in his gut, that gnawing and clenching. When Jayden first found out how much the new Kendrick Kings cost—$130, plus tax—he'd put the thought of ever owning them far from his mind. Now that they were on his feet, he was thrilled, of course. But the heaviness of knowing how hard his mother must have had to work to afford them was beginning to overshadow the thrill of owning the coolest shoes on the market.

Jayden sat down on his bed and considered taking the shoes off and telling his mother to return them. Then he noticed an index card on top of the packing paper inside the shoebox. His name and the date were at the top in his mother's handwriting. Below, it read:

Son, I love you more than you will ever know, and I believe in you more than you will ever know. Whether you want to play in the NBA like Kendrick King or fly to the moon, you have the potential to do all that and more. When you wear these shoes, I want you to remember that.

Now, seven hours later, Jayden still has the flyest kicks in all of Carter Middle, and even more important, he is just one more class away from Hoop Group. Just fifty-five more minutes of first-day get-to-know-yous and what-to-expects and he'd be able to show all the kids from last year (and some new kids, too) how much his game has improved.

Jayden's last class is Creative Writing, and he's far from thrilled about it. He's not interested in *poetic thinking* or *emotional exploration*, but there is, perhaps, a slight silver lining. If he and his classmates are going to be forced to *find their voices*, at least they don't have to do it until the last period of the day.

As he stops by his locker to drop off his history book and pick up his writing notebook, Jayden nearly bumps into the kid whose locker is right next to his. It is remarkable that Jayden didn't notice him before, unloading and reloading his own backpack, because the kid is *big*. Maybe the biggest kid in the whole school. Jayden remembers seeing him around last year, but not very often and never in any of his own classes.

"My bad," Jayden says. Then, after a beat: "You good?"

The kid studies Jayden's face as if contemplating the sincerity of his apology, as if trying to decide whether it merits an actual response. His eyes then soften with recognition. "You play basketball, right?" he says. "With Hoop Group?"

"Yeah, I do," Jayden says, immediately at ease. "I'm Jayden, by the way."

"Cool. I'm Anthony. I thought you looked familiar." He pauses, looks down at his feet. "Hoop Group practice starts today, right?"

"Yeah," Jayden says, confused. "Today's the first day."

Basketball is Jayden's whole life, and he probably knows every other kid his age who plays around town. He definitely knows all the kids at Carter Middle who'd be trying out for Hoop Group, and Anthony definitely isn't one of them. That's not to say the team couldn't use him, though. With his size, Anthony looks like he could easily pass for a high school sophomore.

"I didn't know you hooped," Jayden adds.

Anthony's head dips lower. "I don't. Well, I didn't." A pause with a sigh. "I got into a situation last year. . . ."

"A situation?"

"A fight, I guess. Well, yeah, it was a fight. I got into it with this kid in the cafeteria and it was a whole thing and now I kinda don't have a choice about basketball. Well, not kinda. I *don't* have a choice."

Jayden's wheels are spinning as he listens to Anthony talk, and finally, he remembers. He wasn't in the cafeteria when it happened, when Anthony blasted Tyson Rowley in front of half the sixth grade, but he certainly heard about it. Within minutes, the news tore through the Carter Middle School hallways. Jayden got the story from Sophia Cannon, who's had a crush on him since fourth grade and, as a result, makes it her business to keep Jayden updated on everyone else's.

First, Anthony asked for Tyson's bologna sandwich, then his homework, then his phone, Sophia said, her head swiveling right to left like a real-life SMH hashtag. *Tyson just handed*

25

everything right on over, too. Didn't say a thing and probably woulda given Anthony the shoes on his feet if he woulda asked. Crazy thing is, the more Tyson gave him, the madder Anthony got.

Jayden kept nodding and *mm-hmm*ing in all the right spots, and Sophia just kept talking, yapping away like she was an anchor on the evening news. *By the time Tyson slid his iPhone across the table to Anthony, ya boy had had enough, okay? One hit laid Tyson out, and I mean* smooth out. *Principal Kim had to come break up the fight, but between me and you—* Sophia said this as if it were really a private conversation between the two of them and not school-wide gossip—*it wasn't no fight. Not at all. Tyson never had a chance.*

Jayden looks at Anthony now, all 5'10" and 175 pounds of him, and immediately understands how he could overwhelm a kid like Tyson—or any other kid. He also decides to stay on Anthony's good side.

"I heard about that," Jayden says.

"Yeah, you and everybody else in this school." Anthony shrugs. "It's cool now, though. Tyson's parents wanted me expelled, but Dr. Kim gave me another chance. She just said I gotta join Hoop Group to 'put my anger and energy into something productive.'"

Jayden can't help but laugh when Anthony throws up his air quotes.

With another shrug, Anthony pulls a notebook from his locker that is identical to Jayden's. He also pulls out a copy of *The Collected Poems of Langston Hughes.* When Anthony catches Jayden looking at it, he quickly slips it into his backpack.

"Creative Writing?" Jayden says. "That's where I'm going, too."

"I guess that makes three of us," a voice says from behind Jayden.

Jayden turns around and finds Chris King smiling wide and leaning against a nearby locker. "I see you got the new KKs," he says, pointing at the black-white-and-gold shoes on Jayden's feet. He crosses his arms in front of his chest and nods with an air of artificial authority. "I knew those colors would look the best. Uncle Ken was trying to decide between a black-and-red or a silver-and-white version, but I told him to go with those. I can't lie, though, the black-and-red ones are fresh. I got a pair at the house."

"Ah yeah?" Anthony says, stepping into the conversation. "Why you got on them busted kicks from last year, then?"

Jayden struggles to keep his laugh to himself. Since third grade, Chris has based his entire personality on the fact that he's Kendrick King's nephew. It was cool at first, back when everybody was eight. Now it's just old and annoying, especially since Chris's bloodline has done very little for his basketball abilities.

Chris's cheeks flush beneath his khaki-colored skin, and he looks around to see if anybody else heard the diss. "I, uh . . . I keep all my new KKs locked in a safe at my house. I ain't tryin to mess 'em up, you know what I'm sayin'?"

Unimpressed, Anthony shakes his head, hits Chris with a "yeah, right," and turns to head toward Creative Writing, leaving Jayden and Chris alone in the hallway.

There is a moment between the two boys, a break in the conversation just long enough for them to size each other up, to try and get a sense of how the summer break changed the other.

"You playing in Hoop Group this year?" Chris asks, his posture now upright and defiant.

"Yeah," Jayden says, adjusting his body language to match Chris's. "You?"

Chris chuckles. "You already know. I been waiting on this day for months."

Jayden feels a pang of nervousness rip through him,

as if Chris's confidence is an attack on his own game. But then he remembers Roddy's words and shakes it off. "All right, bet," he says. "I guess I'll see you out there, then."

"Cool."

"Cool."

CHAPTER 4

AS ANTHONY ENTERS the Carter Middle School gym, the sound of the squeaking sneakers on the old parquet floor is enough to immediately knot his insides. He has no interest in basketball and no idea how to play, and he's been trying to explain that to people for the last two years. Ever since he grew four inches the summer after he turned ten, he's been approached by one stranger after another who likes to guess that he plays basketball or football, maybe both. It's the Lorain way, after all, to assume a kid with Anthony's size would take to sports, so Anthony typically just nods and smiles at the old men with gray hair and calloused hands as they prophesy that

he could be the next Bill Russell or, better yet, Refrigerator Perry. But Anthony doesn't want to be the next Bill
Russell or Refrigerator Perry. Truth be told, he doesn't
even know who they are. All he knows is that he's been
stuck with the worst punishment in the history of Carter
Middle School punishments.

Anthony still remembers the day he and his mom were
seated across from Principal Kim in her office, how she
drew her lips into a tight frown and told them that, while
she didn't believe in expulsion, Anthony would still have
to face the consequences of his actions. Hoop Group, she
believed, would provide structure and discipline, even if
Anthony didn't know the difference between a screen and
a press. The only issue was that, since the fight with Tyson
had happened during the second week of May, basketball
season, like most of the school year, was already over. As
a result, Anthony's punishment was set to begin the following fall—which meant Anthony's entire summer had
been one long countdown to the start of school and, with
it, the start of Hoop Group.

Since there was no way of getting out of Hoop Group,
Anthony quickly devised a plan for survival. He'd keep

out of trouble and do just enough to stay in the program without actually becoming, well, a *basketball player*. Principal Kim's only requirement was that Anthony be present in the gym from 3:00 p.m. until 5:00 every day. She never said anything about him being any good.

Anthony's eyes skip across the court, bouncing over the focused expressions of all the other kids taking practice shots and likely planning their acceptance speeches for their first NBA MVP win. He rolls his eyes. Even though he knew he'd be out of place, Anthony realizes he'd completely underestimated the seriousness of middle school basketball. The kids are determined, deliberate, and, in some cases, really, really good.

In other cases . . . not so much.

As Anthony begins making his way over to Jayden, the only person he knows in the whole gym, he sidesteps a glasses-wearing kid who is half his size and trying to dribble through a maze of orange traffic cones. Not only is the kid wearing an obnoxious stick-on name tag that reads MY NAME IS DEXTER in bold red Sharpie, but he also seems just as bad at basketball as Anthony. After a couple of dribbles, the ball careens wildly off Dexter's foot, forcing him to go chasing after it.

Anthony watches Dexter run off before turning his attention back to Jayden, who's stretching in the far corner of the gym. Anthony is nearly close enough to speak when he stops short, suddenly distracted. Just a few feet in front of him is the most beautiful girl he's ever seen.

Anthony feels his breath catch. The girl is tall with long copper-colored legs that stretch out from beneath royal-blue Nike shorts; her hair is gathered into a mass of dark brown curls atop her head; and in the thirty seconds Anthony has been standing, staring, she hasn't missed one single shot.

"Who is that?" Anthony asks once he finally reaches Jayden.

Jayden exhales as he pulls his right foot behind him to stretch the front of his thigh. "Who is who?"

Anthony points just as the girl drains a three from at least four steps beyond the arc. *"Her."*

Jayden follows Anthony's finger, sees the girl he's also been watching since she first stepped foot inside the gym, and shrugs. "No clue. I heard somebody say her name was Tamika, but I've never seen her before."

Having a new kid at Hoop Group practice was note-worthy enough, but Tamika's presence was particularly significant. When Coach Beck created the program some twenty-eight years before, he was explicit about Hoop Group rules: Players were to operate in excellence on the court and off, teammates were to be treated like family members, and, finally, Hoop Group was for boys only.

He'd never say it out loud, by Jayden always felt that the No Girls Allowed rule was less archaic than it sounded. Boys' basketball teams had always been kept separate from girls' teams, and Hoop Group just happened to be for the Carter Middle School boys. It was just the way things were. Sure, the girls' program at the school had folded a decade ago, and even when it was still in opera-tion, it never came close to achieving the recognition that Hoop Group did. But Jayden never thought it was a prob-lem that girls couldn't play with Hoop Group. He didn't even know any girls who *wanted* to.

That is, until he saw Tamika.

Now, as Jayden watches her glide across the floor and sink nine jump shots in a row, Coach Beck's rule does seem a bit ridiculous. Tamika definitely looks like she can hold her own against anyone. In fact, Jayden can think of at least six kids from last year's team who Tamika would absolutely demolish in a one-on-one. *It's just too bad,* Jayden thinks to himself, *'cause Coach Beck is never gonna let her play.*

Aside from the mandates on performance, loyalty, and gender, there is one other Hoop Group rule, and it is this: Early is on time, and on time is late. It is a surprise, then, that when Coach Beck finally shows up for practice, the large clock on the gym's north wall reads 3:19. Still, no one seems to be concerned about Coach Beck's uncharacteristic tardiness. As soon as he walks onto the court, everyone knows it's time for the annual Day One Court Run.

The anxious energy in the room is palpable as the kids await the moment when Coach Beck will pick captains and send them off with their teams. Jayden can hardly stand still as he prays that his name will be called first, that the first day of his seventh-grade season will begin just as he dreamed it would all summer long. But when Coach opens his mouth to speak, Jayden is shocked by the words that come tumbling out. Coach Beck doesn't announce the first captain; instead, he tells everyone to take a seat on the bleachers so he can share something important.

The request is strange, coming at the beginning of what should be two full hours of back-to-back games, but the kids take their seats as instructed. After a few seconds of throat clearing and brow wiping, Coach is ready to begin.

"I know you guys are looking forward to today's run, and to the rest of the season, but I have an announcement that I need to make." He sighs heavily and shoves both hands deep into the pockets of his sweatpants. "This has been a really rough summer for me, personally, and I'm afraid I'm not going to be able to coach Hoop Group this year."

There is a collective gasp that ripples across the bleachers. Then, as Coach Beck's words linger in the air, stunned silence turns into a low hum of whispers. One by one each kid turns to another and another, trying to make sense of it all.

"I'm going to be okay," Coach says finally. "But—"

Coach's words stop as his gaze locks with Jayden's. Jayden can't help but notice that Coach's eyes look glassy and distant, as if he's just been crying. In response,

Jayden feels his chest start to rise and fall, rise and fall, and his brain starts spinning likes Grams's old washing machine. *What more could there be? What else is there left to say?*

". . . But without a coach," Coach Beck continues, "Hoop Group can't continue. You'll still have access to the courts, but there will be no official team, and there will be no real season this year."

That's it.

The death knell, the worst-case scenario. Seventh grade might as well be over, and no one—absolutely *no one*—saw it coming.

The next minutes unfold in slow motion. Coach asks the kids if there are any questions, and he is immediately met with a chorus of anguish and despair. There are so many voices calling out at once that Coach Beck must wave his arms in surrender and shout loud above the din: "One person at a time!"

The first person he calls on is a kid who, conveniently, has a name tag stuck to the front of his tank top. "Yes, Dexter," Coach Beck says.

Jayden watches as the kid smiles awkwardly and pushes his glasses up on his nose. "Actually, I go by Dex, and I was just wondering: you said there won't be a season this year, so does that mean we can't play in the Fall Invitational?"

Coach sighs. "No season means no season, and no season means no Fall Invitational. I'm sorry about that. I know a lot of you were looking forward to playing against the top programs in the state and hopefully getting on the radar of some of the big prep schools, but there's just nothing I can do."

Dex asks a few follow-up questions—*Is there another coach or teacher who can come in to help out? Maybe a parent, even? If we get another coach, can Hoop Group continue?*—but all the words seem to collide and scramble inside Jayden's brain. Nothing that Coach says matters anymore, and neither, it seems to Jayden, do his dreams.

Jayden's frustration is morphing into anger, and as he looks around at the other kids—kids whose moms probably have their own beds—he knows it's impossible that anyone could have loved Hoop Group more than him, could have longed for this season more than him, and could be, in this heartbreaking moment, more devastated than him.

Jayden is tempted to walk out of the gym right then, to

run away and never come back, but before he can, he is interrupted by movement on the far end of the bleachers. He cranes his neck just in time to see Tamika jump up from her seat and grab her backpack. All eyes look in her direction, but she turns her back to the group as she hurries out of the gym. It's too late, though. Jayden already saw the tears that are streaming down her cheeks.

CHAPTER 5

IN THE GIRLS' BATHROOM just adjacent to the gym, Tamika splashes cold water on her cheeks and takes several slow, deep breaths. She grabs a paper towel and blots her face, trying to make herself look presentable again, but her efforts do nothing for her puffy, reddened eyes. As if her reflection weren't pitiful enough, she also can't decide whether she's more bothered by her father's announcement or the fact that she allowed herself to break down in front of all those boys. It's the first day of Hoop Group, and here she is, the only girl, *crying*.

Tamika was only a week into summer break when her mother told her that she wouldn't be able to go back to

Austinberg Prep, that she needed Tamika at home, with the rest of the family.

Tamika's response was anger and resistance—a notable departure from the fit she threw when her parents first suggested that she go to Austinberg. She was just a fifth grader then, just ten years old, but Coach Beck and her mom were adamant about getting Tamika out of Lorain and into the best school possible. Austinberg was two hundred miles away, and Tamika's early homesickness was almost unbearable. Soon, though, she discovered that she felt more welcome and free to be herself at Austinberg than she did in most other places.

At Austinberg, Tamika met a dozen other girls just like her—smart and competitive and in love with the game of basketball. Her first year there, Tamika was one of twelve girls who made the fifth-and-sixth-grade travel team out of the thirty who tried out. By her second year, last year, Tamika was named captain. And along with Charlene, a six-foot-tall forward with guard-like ball-handling skills, she led the team to a 22-2 record. The season ended on a sour note—one of those losses came during the last game, when a team from Cleveland beat Tamika's team by twenty-five—but as soon as the final buzzer sounded, all the girls began looking forward to the next year, to seventh grade. That was the year they'd be able to play with the eighth graders and compete against other middle school prep teams for the regional and national title. It was going to be an unprecedented season. The news that she couldn't be a part of it was like a dagger through Tamika's chest.

Tamika's pleading was incessant until, finally, her mother told her the real reason she wasn't allowed to go back to Austinberg: *Your father has Parkinson's*, she'd said. *He was diagnosed some time ago, but we didn't want to tell you because we didn't want you to be scared. I'm only telling you now because he's getting worse and I think you should be home so that you can spend as much time with him as possible before things . . . change.*

In that moment, Tamika closed her eyes and saw an imaginary headline from the sports page of the *Lorain Herald*:

Coach Richard Beck Diagnosed with Parkinson's Disease: Founder of Carter Middle School's Hoop Group and Mentor to Kendrick King Said to be "Getting Worse"

The only solace Tamika had found in leaving Austinberg was the hope that she'd be able to join her dad's team.

Yes, Hoop Group had always been a boys-only program, but since Coach Beck was suffering from an incurable disease, Tamika figured that he might not care too much about enforcing such an outdated rule. Never once did she consider that he wouldn't be coaching at all.

Then came the announcement in front of all those kids. Now, claiming a spot on the team is the least of Tamika's concerns. If her father is giving up Hoop Group—the thing he loves most of all; more, she sometimes believes, than her—he must be in worse shape than she thought.

Ten minutes later, Tamika's face is a little less flushed, her eyes a little less puffy. She decides to head back into the gym, and she arrives just as Coach Beck says he's ready to choose team captains.

Confused, she asks Dex for an update. He tells her that, although Coach Beck still hasn't provided any real answers about what will happen to the program or why he's stepping down, Coach did agree to oversee the Day One Court Run. Normally, the elimination-style tournament pits teams of three against each other to help determine which kids need to tighten up their games and which ones are most likely to snag the season's starting positions. With Hoop Group canceled for the year, pride is the only prize up for grabs.

Tamika turns away from Dex as she feels overcome with gratitude. Just minutes before, she was a crying mess preparing to pack up her things and head home. Now there's a chance to redeem herself—perhaps the only chance, she realizes, to show all the boys that she belongs. This is her moment, and that moment starts with being chosen as a team captain.

First, Coach Beck calls for volunteers. Tamika immediately shoves her hand into the air, as do Jayden and Chris. After seeing Jayden during shootaround, Tamika considers him a logical choice. But Chris? It only took two seconds watching him play to see that he was all swag with little skill. Tamika's not really sure Chris belongs on the court at all, but it's obvious that the other kids disagree.

Tamika can hear them as they whisper: *He's Kendrick King's nephew; he should* definitely *be captain.* And: *I hope Chris picks me first, for real. Maybe he can introduce me to his uncle!*

Coach Beck is silently deliberating, and the longer he takes, the more Tamika knows she's not going to be happy with his decision. Sure enough, Chris is named the first captain, and as he saunters to the sideline, Coach Beck points at Jayden. Four more names are called next, and still none of them are Tamika's. Coach Beck doesn't even look his daughter in the eye as she stands there, dejected.

Tamika is still seething as the teams are decided, as Chris chooses her nearly last, adding another chip to her slumping shoulders. It takes everything in her to push aside the sting of rejection and step into competition mode, but she does it anyway. She has no choice.

Chris and Tamika's first matchup is against Jayden, whose squad includes Dex and a really big kid named Anthony. When they hit the court, Jayden seems hesitant to step into his role as a captain, and his team gets off to a slow start. Meanwhile, on Tamika's half of the floor, her captain is more than willing to take charge, even though he's clearly unqualified. Aside from being weak inside, Chris lacks finesse. He's trying too hard to be a star, and he repeatedly overshoots, clanging the ball loudly against the backboard.

About five minutes in, with Tamika's team down 10–2, she decides to step up and take charge. She may not be the captain, but she refuses to stand by as her team gets demolished.

On back-to-back fast breaks, Tamika drives to the hole, spins around defenders, and banks two easy layups. New score: 10–6.

On the other team's next possession, Tamika is squared up against Jayden, determined to prevent him from getting another bucket. She guards him close but respects his speed enough to give him a little space so that he doesn't blow past her. She watches his eyes, sees him search for his teammates and then second-guess, realizing that if the team is going to score, it's going to be up to him.

Jayden starts to dribble to his left, but Tamika knows it's a fake. Just as he breaks back to the right, she backs up two steps to cut off the angle she knows he's going to take to the basket. Sure enough, Jayden pushes into the lane, and Tamika is right there, arms high. Jayden goes up for the shot, but Tamika brings her right hand down at the same time, knocking the ball from Jayden's hand and sending him hard to the floor.

It was a foul, but it was a good, clean foul—even if Jayden isn't happy about it.

Jayden is rattled, his confidence clearly bruised. And

when his team gets the ball back, he is unable to regain his composure. He starts driving into traffic, forcing up ill-advised shots, and committing dumb reach-in fouls. Ultimately, his reckless play turns a game they should have easily won into a lopsided loss.

After the game, Jayden is alone on the bleachers, clearly humbled, when Coach Beck comes and sits next to him.

"You looked good out there," Coach Beck says.

Jayden's face twists with confusion. "We lost."

"You're right. You did lose. But you didn't lose because of your game. You lost because of your emotions."

Jayden drops his head and studies the dimples on the basketball balanced between his knees.

"Your shot is so much better than it was last year," Coach continues. "You're seeing the whole floor now, and you're able to adjust to defenders on the fly. All of that's important. But do you see how important it is that you also keep your head in the game?"

Jayden nods silently.

"Listen, son. You're probably the kid I was most looking forward to coaching this year." Coach pauses, takes a slow breath. "I hate that I'm not going to be here, but I want you to hear what I'm saying."

Jayden looks up and meets Coach Beck eye-to-eye, man-to-man.

"I don't know what's going to happen with Hoop Group, but I want you to stick with it. You have the potential to go far. Really far. And as far as I'm concerned, you are Hoop Group captain. So even though I won't be here, if this program is going to continue, it's going to be with you. I need you to step up and be a leader."

Jayden's heart fills with pride. Even more than the fact that he trained a young Kendrick King, the thing about Coach Beck that impresses Jayden is his basketball IQ. Coach knows the game inside and out, so when he says that he sees something special in Jayden, it carries extra weight. The season's status is uncertain, but for Jayden, Coach Beck's compliment may be the highlight of the year.

As Coach Beck heads to the locker room, Jayden gathers his ball and his backpack and begins walking toward the gym doors. On his way, he looks over at Tamika, who is taking practice shots from the free-throw line. He nods in her direction, but she ignores him, reserving her attention and energy for the rim.

Jayden doesn't realize it, but Tamika overheard every word of his conversation with Coach Beck. And now that she knows that Coach Beck has crowned Jayden Hoop Group captain instead of his own daughter—his daughter who just single-handedly beat Jayden's team—the fury that began its slow simmer in Tamika's chest during the Day One Court Run is threatening to boil over.

Tamika has so much to prove, but with Hoop Group's future up in the air, she's not sure that she'll have the chance.

CHAPTER 6

WHEN HOOP GROUP ENDS FOR THE DAY, uncertainty hangs heavy, and most of the kids wonder whether they'll spend the upcoming season playing their own games or cheering for someone else's. For now, though, Chris King is just happy to go home—even if he has to talk basketball with his dad the whole way.

Chris's dad, Cam, showed up to watch the last few minutes of the Day One Court Run games. While there, he got the full scoop on Coach's forced retirement, and he's already thinking of ways to capitalize on it.

"Hoop Group's been around a long time, but I can't see it surviving this," Cam says to Chris as soon as he pulls his Toyota Camry out of the Carter Middle School parking lot. "I'mma say this, too: Your future ain't bout to be ruined just cause Old Man Beck had to step down. You feel me?"

Cam eases the sedan into the evening rush-hour traffic and continues. "This is your seventh-grade year. It's serious now. And if you think you belong at Willow Brook, now's the time for you to show it."

Chris sits on his hands and remains silent. He's honestly not sure where he belongs, but when his father turns to him, expecting a response, he nods and says "yes, sir" anyway.

"Cool. 'Cause I got a plan."

Suddenly, Chris's abdomen feels as though someone is wringing it like a wet dish rag. "What kinda plan?"

"That's for me to worry about, not you," his dad says, chuckling. "Just trust that I'mma make sure everybody knows how much of a star you are."

Chris shifts uncomfortably in his seat. The first day of Hoop Group clearly showed that he was far from being the best kid on the court. On top of that, he's not even sure he wants to be a basketball star. But none of that matters, of course—not when your last name is King.

Chris looks over at his father, sees his jaw muscles tighten, the wheels in his brain turning round and round. He thinks about the stories his dad has told him about his childhood, how he used to hoop back in the day but never got the love that Kendrick did. Even though Kendrick is four years younger, Cam spent much of his youth waiting backstage while his little brother, with talent and charisma oozing from every pore, soaked up all the spotlight. He's never admitted it, but Chris knows that his dad has never recovered from those slights. It's obvious in the way he's spent his whole life trying to prove himself.

Chris's father steers onto Piedmont Boulevard through the heart of downtown Lorain, past the empty buildings with FOR LEASE and FOR SALE posters in the windows, past a giant sign that reads #LongLiveLorain. The hashtag is the slogan of a new organization dedicated to revitalizing Lorain's economy and encouraging people to shop locally. The signs are all over town—big and bright and covered in cheery green and yellow paint—and Chris can't help but wonder why they didn't use some of the sign money to replace the broken basketball hoops at Garvey Park instead.

"Listen," his dad says, "I was watching y'all play, and if I'mma be honest, nobody out there was better than you. I mean, you got in your head a little bit, but you still had the purest game, you feel me? That Jayden kid was a mess. He was just jacking up shots 'cause he let that girl . . . Um . . . What's her name again?"

"Tamika."

"Yeah, Tamika. Jayden let Tamika throw him off his game. He definitely ain't a star, I'mma tell you that. And Tamika—" Chris's dad laughs, shakes his head. "I don't know how she thinks she's gonna hang with a bunch of dudes. But whatever."

Chris's stomach twists again.

"What I'm saying is, you don't need none of those scrubs."

Chris swallows hard and looks at his father's face, all hard and stern. He knows better than to argue. "Yeah, Pop," he says, fake-smiling and nodding. "I feel you."

Chris has no idea what his father has in store; all he can do is hope that it doesn't turn out as badly as his last "great idea." It's been three years since his dad roped Kendrick into a shady deal selling knockoff jerseys, three years since Cam had to do six months in jail for concocting the scheme, and three years since Kendrick last spoke to Cam—or to Chris.

A block and a half from Carter Middle, in an apartment complex buried under decades' worth of disrepair, Dex slides his hand down the front of his T-shirt and retrieves the key that is dangling from a long black shoestring fastened loosely around his neck. He slides the key into the lock, turns the knob, and, with a firm shove from his shoulder, forces the door open. Dex can't ever remember a time when the door didn't stick or, for that matter, when their landlord has ever come to fix a single thing in their apartment. In the meantime, he and his mom have learned to make do. A stiff push pops the door; a utility bucket catches the drip in the bathroom; a piece of wide silver duct tape keeps the oven's door from falling open.

Inside his apartment, Dex retrieves his mother's old flip phone from the utility drawer in the kitchen. When he opens the device and sees 5:24 blinking back at him, his heart drops into his stomach. Dex's mom gets a thirty-minute lunch and two ten-minute breaks when she works a full shift at Top Burger. Over the summer, they agreed that if Dex was going to play with Hoop Group this year, she'd schedule her second break for 5:20 every day. That way, she'd be able to answer the phone when Dex calls to let her know that he's made it home from school safely. But today, he's late. Four minutes late, to be exact.

"Hi, Mom," Dex says as soon as he hears his mother's voice on the other end on the phone.

Dex's mother sighs heavily into the phone.

"Mom, I'm sorry. Today was the first day and there was a lot of drama at practice, so I didn't get to leave right at five. Really. Coach Beck came late, and then he stepped down, and—"

"It's fine, Dex," she says, cutting him off. "I understand. I'm just . . . I'm just tired, that's all."

She stops talking long enough for Dex to hear Ms. Felicia, one of his mom's coworkers, remind her that she has only a few minutes left on her break. Felicia says she needs a smoke and Adam, their supervisor, won't let her leave the register until she comes back. Dex's mom mumbles that she'll be right there, and Dex's face warms with shame.

"Listen, I gotta go," she says, turning her attention back to her son, "but you know the drill: Don't answer the door, don't invite anyone over, and make sure you keep the TV on."

"I know, Mom."

Ever since the break-in at Mrs. Bailey's apartment, Dex's mom has been worried that someone will force their way into their place while she's away at work. They don't have any family or friends nearby who can keep an eye on Dex when he gets home from school, and Dex's mom certainly can't afford to work part-time hours. The only alternative is to keep the volume inside the apartment loud enough that potential burglars may be scared off—and for Dex to become a master at getting his homework done while the TV drones away in the background.

"Okay, baby," Dex's mom says just before she hangs up. "I gotta study for my biology test when I get home, but before that, I want you to tell me all about the first day of Hoop Group. Okay?"

"Okay," Dex says.

"All right. Love you. See you soon."

Dex claps the phone shut and returns it to the drawer. He then pulls a one-pound tube of ground beef from the refrigerator and a box of Hamburger Helper from the cabinet. On Fridays, his mom sometimes brings burgers from the restaurant. Every other weekday, including today, Dex is responsible for his own dinner. His mom doesn't get home till around 8:00, so if he doesn't feed himself, he'll surely starve. Even then, between the nine-hour shifts at Top Burger and the constant studying for her associate's degree at Lorain Community College, Dex's mom simply doesn't have time to cook.

She was just sixteen when Dex was born. Deciding to drop out of Carter High was easy, considering how little she cared about school in the first place. But years later, when Dex was starting school himself, she decided to get her GED. She'd already learned that finding a decent job without a high school diploma was incredibly difficult, that raising a kid on minimum wage and minimal family support was nearly impossible.

Dex still remembers his mom squeezing in time to study for her GED when she wasn't working as a janitor at Carter. There were days when he just knew she'd give up—when Dex was sick with the flu, or she was sick herself, or the humiliation of scrubbing toilets at her old high school threatened to overtake her—but she never did.

Dex's mom didn't have a lot of money to celebrate when she finally passed and her certificate came in the mail a few weeks later, but she did splurge for double cheese-burgers and strawberry milkshakes from Top Burger. A few months later, she began working on an associate's of Applied Science in Nursing.

Between work and school, the days are long for Dex's mom, so he considers his boxed beef Stroganoff a small price compared to the daily sacrifices she makes to build a better life for them both. The bigger problem for Dex is finding a way to fill all the hours he spends by himself.

It wasn't always like this, this being alone. He used to walk home from school with a group of kids that also lived in his complex, but as Dex began taking an interest in basketball and his friends began skipping their home-work—and then skipping school altogether—they all grew apart. Now, instead of spending afternoons playing video games or running errands for some of the older guys in the complex, Dex turns to YouTube.

As soon as his homework is done, Dex streams old basketball games in an endless loop on the old desktop computer they bought for sixty-five dollars from Lucky's Pawn Shop. It's not in great shape, but with a solid inter-net connection, it works perfectly fine for watching old film of the Cleveland Cavaliers. And Dex has watched a lot.

He's watched enough interviews and game film to consider anyone who's ever been on the Cavs a close friend. He's also discovered that there's a Cav era for his every mood: There's the 1970 Cavs for the dose of hope and excitement that newness brings; there's Austin "Mr. Cavalier" Carr's late-'70s Cavs for the days when it feels like all you have is never enough; and there's the early-90s Cavs, with Mark Price and Brad Daugherty to remind you that anything is, indeed, possible.

So in the moments when dusk turns to night—when Dex's books are returned to his backpack for school the next day and he's covered his mom's dinner portion in foil—he settles in and lets Joe Tait broadcasting from the Richfield Coliseum keep him company until he's no longer alone.

CHAPTER 7

THE CLOCK ON THE GYM WALL reads 3:06, and Chris, Dex, Anthony, Jayden, and Tamika are the only players who have shown up for the second day of not-quite-Hoop-Group. Without Coach Beck's leadership, they all stand in awkward silence, waiting for someone to step up and take charge. Miss Turner, a sixth-grade TA, has been assigned to monitor any basketball activity. Based on the stack of papers she's busy grading, she has no intention of actually getting involved.

After a few more moments of sideways glances, Tamika walks to the middle of the court, her right foot resting firmly on the beak of the Carter Middle mascot—a cardinal—that is painted there.

"I'm appointing myself captain of Hoop Group," she says matter-of-factly.

Jayden shifts his weight from one leg to another, but ultimately says nothing. Chris, on the other hand, speaks up immediately.

"How are you automatically the captain?" he says.

Tamika rolls her eyes. "Do you have another option? I waited for almost ten minutes for one of you to say something, but since you didn't, I did."

Dex and Anthony look at each other, and then away.

"Maybe we should vote," Chris says. "How do you know I don't wanna be captain?"

Tamika rolls her eyes again but concedes. "Fine. Let's vote. Everybody who wants me to be captain, raise your hand."

Anthony's hand is up in an instant. Jayden hesitates— he doesn't want Tamika *or* Chris to be captain—but he waits too long. Dex raises his hand in favor of Tamika, too.

"Two out of three!" Tamika says. "Jayden's vote doesn't even matter."

Tamika shoots an I-told-you-so look in Chris's direction

and continues. "Now, as long as we're all here, we might as well play and at least try to get better as a team. I think we should start with a game of two-on-two so we can see what everybody needs to work on. Jayden and Anthony against Chris and Dex. I'll referee."

After speaking, Tamika looks over at Miss Turner, who still hasn't lifted her head. With no objection, she tosses the ball to Chris. "Y'all take it out first."

There is a moment when it seems like Chris is going to push back again, that he's going to assert some flimsy claim born of his famous last name, but he thinks better of it and heads to the baseline. Jayden tells Anthony to slide over to guard Chris while he squares up against Dex. Seconds later, the game is underway.

The teams are as even as they can be, given the circumstances, and Tamika watches from the sideline as Jayden falls into an easy rhythm. He is confident but calm, playing nothing like he did just one day prior. At the same time, Chris is serving up more of the same.

On defense, Chris takes Jayden, and from the beginning, it's clear that he's outmatched. First, Jayden hits a couple of mid-range jumpers, stepping back just enough to rise up high above Chris's outstretched arms. Frustrated,

Chris starts playing him tighter, and Tamika shakes her head at what she knows is coming next. Jayden blows past Chris, taking it straight to the hole.

Now Chris is embarrassed and struggling, so he starts flopping, calling imaginary fouls, and accusing Jayden of traveling, double-dribbling, carrying . . . anything to mask his own deficiencies. But Tamika's in charge, and she waves Chris off, telling him that Jayden is playing clean, that he needs to slide faster on his feet and figure out how to cut off the drive. It doesn't matter, though. Chris keeps whining and complaining anyway.

"Look, man," Jayden finally says to him, "if you don't wanna play, just say that."

Chris huffs and crosses his arms at his chest. "Oh, so I'm not supposed to say something when you take an extra step on every layup? That's called a *travel.*"

"Travel?! Man, whatever. You just mad 'cause you keep getting *beat.*"

"So I'm getting beat? That's what you think?" Chris takes two steps forward—just enough to position himself two inches from Jayden's face.

Jayden calls Chris's bluff and stands firm. "Nah, man. That's what I *know.* And it's a shame your uncle ain't here to save you from this *beating*."

In an instant, Miss Turner stands up from her seat ready to jump in, but from Tamika's vantage point, Chris's fist is sure to connect with Jayden's jaw before she'll ever have time to reach them. Then, just as Chris begins to curl his fingers tight—just before he can redeem his name and his tattered game—Anthony has positioned himself between the two boys. With one quick motion he shoves Chris back at least ten yards.

Chris takes a couple of breaths, regains his balance, and wipes dripping sweat from his brow. "You know what," Chris says, his voice inexplicably cocky. "My dad was right. Y'all some scrubs. I'm done with this."

He walks to the far end of the court, picks up his backpack, and, without saying another word, exits the gym. Tamika is stunned, but before she has time to take control, Jayden has gathered his things and is halfway out the gym, too.

"Where are you going?" Tamika calls after him.

Jayden shakes his head and continues walking. "I'm going home. Hoop Group ain't supposed to be like this."

The door closes behind Jayden and silence settles over the gym. Tamika can feel Anthony and Dex staring at her, waiting on her to do something, to say anything.

But what is there to say? Or do? Tamika looks up at the clock. 3:42. Just two hours and 42 minutes into the season and Hoop Group is down to three players.

CHAPTER 8

IT'S BEEN EIGHT DAYS since Jayden and Chris's fight when Chris strolls into Ms. Cahill's Creative Writing class smiling wide and clutching a shopping bag loaded with full-sized Snickers bars wrapped in neon-green paper. In the few minutes before class starts, Chris begins making his way around the room, sidling up to each of the boys like a politician campaigning for votes. First, he stops at the desk belonging to a kid named Carlos.

"Yo," Chris says, handing Carlos a candy bar, "my dad started a new basketball program called the Ballers. We practice every afternoon at the Lorain YMCA. You should come check it out."

As soon as he hears this, Jayden looks up from the math homework he's hoping to finish before the end of the school day. Carlos has never played a sport and is well known as the kid who took a book to recess during elementary school. Still Chris's assumption that Carlos has suddenly become an athlete is the least surprising part of their exchange. For Jayden, Chris's mention of a basketball program not named Hoop Group has him most intrigued.

As Carlos unwraps his Snickers and takes the first bite, Chris moves over to Anthony and Dex, whose desks have been right next to each other ever since Dex rearranged his schedule and joined their class. Dex and Anthony both gladly accept Chris's offering, but Jayden knows that neither of them will even consider leaving Hoop Group. Even though there's not much of a Hoop Group left, Anthony is bound to the program by principal decree, Dex by unfailing loyalty.

Finally, Chris reaches Jayden's desk. Jayden wonders if Chris is going to mention their last interaction in the gym—the argument that shattered the already weakened team—but Chris, ever the showman, smiles even wider. "Come check it out," he tells Jayden. "First practice is free."

First practice is free.

There has never been a cost to join Hoop Group, and Jayden, puzzled, rips the flyer off the Snickers. He scans the page until his eyes land on *$200*, typed in bold print. His chest deflates like a two-week-old helium balloon. While he was far from happy about the idea of playing with Chris again, he misses basketball so much that he would have at least considered it. The price, however, renders that consideration pointless. There's no way he can ask his mom for $200 to join the Ballers—not after she just dropped nearly that much on his new shoes.

Having suddenly lost his appetite, Jayden tucks the candy bar and the flyer into his backpack as Ms. Cahill signals that class is about to begin.

"It's time to start thinking about your first big writing assignment of the year, and you'll be happy to know that there are very few rules," she says. "You can write about whatever you want, in whatever form you want: essay, poem, letter, story. I don't care. All I ask is that you write about something that is close to your heart."

Some of the kids let out low groans at the word "assignment" while others, like Carlos, seem legitimately excited. Jayden is lost somewhere in the middle. He knows he has to keep his grades up if he wants to get into Willow Brook, so he can't blow the project off completely. At the same time, he can't imagine himself ever being excited about a writing assignment.

"Some of you don't sound too enthusiastic," Ms. Cahill continues, "but you may be pleased to know that, before I ask you to start writing, we're going to analyze some different types of writing forms. This process should help you decide which form you like the most and which one will work best with your voice and vision for this assignment."

Jayden watches as she walks over to her desk and picks up a book that looks vaguely familiar. "We're going to start with poetry," she says, "and today I'm going to read from one of the greats: Langston Hughes."

For a few more moments Jayden struggles to recall where he's seen the book, then his mind sparkles with clarity. Ms. Cahill is holding a copy of *The Collected Poems of Langston Hughes*—the same book Anthony had on the first day of school. He is proud of himself for remembering, but when he turns to look at Anthony with shared recognition, Anthony narrows his eyes into sharp slits, as if daring Jayden to divulge his reading habits.

The truth is, Anthony was already looking forward to the writing project, and seeing Ms. Cahill pick up his favorite book only reinforced his expectation. For Anthony, Hughes's words have a way of stilling the storms of his life and making everything right again—so much so that he doesn't mind when Ms. Cahill starts talking about a "dream deferred" while reading the poem "Harlem."

"Harlem" is a fine poem, but it's not Anthony's favorite, not by a long shot. That distinction belongs to "Mother to Son," the poem Anthony always starts with when he sits down to read Hughes. He's read it literally thousands of times, and he has each stanza committed to memory. In fact, every time he looks at his parents—when he sees the fear and pain in his mother's eyes or the anger and shame in his father's—he whispers the first two lines to himself:

Well, son, I'll tell you:

Life for me ain't been no crystal stair.

After Creative Writing, Jayden heads right out the door of Carter Middle and straight to the Blocks. It's what he's done every day for the last week, ever since he walked away from Hoop Group. He hasn't told his mom and Grams that he quit, so he hits the court from 3:00 to 5:00 to make use of the same time, forgoing his early morning workouts in favor of the late-afternoon hours. He's still hooping and still grinding, even if he's not on a real team.

When Jayden arrives after school, it's still early enough that no trouble has started, but he's never alone like he is at dawn. In the afternoons, the Blocks are filled with older players from the neighborhood, the guys who used to ball and thought they had their own ticket to the League. Now they come to prove that they still got it, never mind the soft arms and even softer bellies. They don't bang in the paint like they used to; now their battles are waged on the perimeter, a bunch of former Shaquille O'Neals turned Reggie Miller wannabes.

They still talk trash, though, and Jayden overhears them when they reminisce about playing in their primes, when they talk about how they faced off against Kendrick King and were just as good as him, if not better.

Jayden is sitting on the edge of the court when he notices that, today, Roddy is among the group. Roddy's no pro, but he's definitely in better shape than the rest of the guys. He's running up and down the court while everyone else jogs. He's moving without the ball, slashing by defenders, cutting to the basket. He's extending his long arms to the heavens, calling for the rock down low, and slamming it home. In the end, Roddy's team handles their opponents easily, and once the game is over, he takes a seat next to Jayden.

"What's good?" Roddy says, breathing heavily.

"Not much," Jayden says. "Surprised to see you, though. You're not normally here this time of day."

"I took the day off work, so thought I'd put in some work down here." Roddy takes a long swig from his water bottle and then turns toward Jayden. "The real question is: Why are *you* here? Hasn't Hoop Group started?"

Jayden shrugs, then fills Roddy in on everything that's happened since the beginning of school. He tells him how Coach Beck stepped down and how he got into a fight with Kendrick King's nephew. He even tells him how he walked out of the gym a week ago and never looked back.

When he's done, Jayden searches Roddy's face for empathy, for sympathy, for some confirmation that he made the right decision in leaving a program that seemed broken beyond repair. But Roddy simply waves him off.

"Everything you just told me is an excuse," he tells Jayden. "What happened to your goal of playing at Willow Brook and then playing college ball? How you think you gonna get *there* from *here?*" he says, pointing a stiff index finger toward the cracked asphalt beneath their feet.

Jayden's voice rises with defensiveness. "How can I play in Hoop Group if there's no Hoop Group?"

"Oh, my bad," Roddy says. "I didn't know that the school shut the program down. I thought you said you quit."

Jayden casts his eyes away from Roddy's and shrinks in the silence that settles between them.

"Well, did the school shut the program down, or did you quit?"

"I quit," Jayden says, his voice barely audible.

"That's what I thought. Now, the last time we were here, we talked about you not giving up as soon as an obstacle appears in your way. That time, it was me standing in the lane and blocking your path to the basket, but my point still applies to every other aspect of your life." He stops then and takes a long, pensive look at the court, as if considering his own words.

"If you wanna win," Roddy continues, "if you wanna even have a *chance* to stay in the game, you gotta decide that nothing's gonna stand in your way. And you gotta *keep* deciding. Every day."

While Jayden is at the Blocks, Tamika is at home, discouraged. She can't run a real practice with only three kids, and she's not sure how to convince more kids to join now that her dad is no longer coaching. Part of her wants to quit, too, to just walk away like Jayden and Chris and convince her mom to let her go back to Austinberg.

But there's another part of her, a part that believes the season might not be lost. During practice, Dex spent an hour trying to convince Tamika and Anthony that Hoop Group could still win the Fall Invitational Tournament. His energy and positivity were undeniable, and as he spoke, Tamika felt herself getting sucked in. Then the clock struck 5:00, and she landed back in the real world.

Now, standing in her driveway, Tamika picks up her basketball and tosses it from hand to hand, taking comfort in the cool leather on her palms. She hasn't spoken to her dad much since he said he was stepping away from Hoop Group, but she wonders if maybe now's the time to talk. Maybe he can give her some advice, tell her how she can salvage Hoop Group and her seventh-grade season.

After just one year at Austinberg, Tamika was already getting looks from the Ohio Players, a nationally ranked, high-school-aged AAU team. Playing for that club would be her best shot at getting into South Carolina, UConn, or one of the other top women's college programs, so she can't afford to regress this year. Not when her former teammates are still working, still growing—and probably passing her by.

Tamika sets her ball in the grass so it doesn't roll into the street. She then makes her way to the house, walking through the garage and laundry room and into the kitchen. There she finds Coach Beck sitting at the table with a glass of lemonade and today's copy of the *Lorain Herald*.

"You wanna play HORSE?" Tamika asks cautiously. "I'll let you go first."

Coach Beck glances at her before returning his focus to the paper. "I wish I could, but the doctors say my basketball days are done. You know that."

"C'mon, Dad. I'm sure you can handle a game of HORSE."

"I'm done with basketball, Tamika," he says, his eyes trained on the newspaper page that he is now slowly turning. "Quite honestly, you should be done with basketball, too. You're getting older now, and the courts are no place for a girl like you."

Just like on the first day of Hoop Group, Tamika feels her eyes well with water. And just like on that first day of Hoop Group, when her hopes and dreams were dashed, she keeps the anger that is gathering on her tongue from spilling out. With her mouth clamped shut, she storms outside and starts tossing up three-pointers, draining every one as a flash rainstorm breaks out.

As the sky alights and thunder barrels through the suddenly cool air, Tamika is wrestling with her thoughts and trying to fight the feeling that her father may be right, that her basketball dreams may actually be out of reach. In Lorain, Ohio, Coach Richard Beck is basketball royalty, but he's also Tamika's father. If he doesn't support her, she's not sure who will.

Tamika's older sister, Tasha, never cared much for basketball. Now a freshman at Columbia University studying political science, Tasha was always happier on the sidelines with a pom-pom than she ever was in the game. As a result, she never experienced the tension with their father that Tamika did, never had to tamp down the passion burning in her soul just because it didn't fit within Coach Beck's narrow vision of who and what his daughters could become.

The rain is coming down in sheets when Coach Beck appears in the front doorway trying to call Tamika in, but Tamika refuses to answer. She won't stop shooting. Her tears have blended with the rain, she's soaked to the bone, and she's sad and mad at the world.

When the clouds finally break and the sun peeks out, Tamika slumps to the ground in a heap of frustration . . . and resolve. She's determined to show the world that nothing can stop her. She belongs in Hoop Group, and she's going to take Dex up on his challenge.

Tamika is going to turn Hoop Group, or what's left of it, into a real team. And they are *going* to win the Fall Invitational Tournament.

CHAPTER 9

FIRST THING THE NEXT MORNING, well before classes start, Tamika beelines to Principal Kim's office. With her heart pumping and adrenaline levels soaring, Tamika ignores the fatigue clamping its jaws around her mind and body. She stayed up most of the night writing a draft of the speech that she hopes will save Hoop Group, and delivering that speech is all she cares about.

Her plan was to arrive at Principal Kim's office just as her day is beginning, before she is buried under the day-to-day responsibilities of running a school with 750 students. It is 7:05, twenty-five minutes before the first bell—early enough, Tamika believes. But when Tamika arrives at Principal Kim's office, she is surprised to find her door closed and her voice already in conversation behind it.

Tamika sighs and takes a seat in the waiting area outside the principal's office as she completes one last mental run-through of her argument: *I was the leading scorer on my team last year and the team captain, even though I was one of the youngest girls. I ran the offense and watched film with my coach to help her come up with game strategy. I've been around basketball all my life, and I know I can coach this team . . . if you let me.*

Finally confident that she can convince Principal Kim to let her lead Hoop Group, Tamika looks up to find Anthony walking out of Dr. Kim's office. Principal Kim is walking with him, and Tamika overhears her say something about "probation" and "continuing to channel his anger."

She stands to her feet as Principal Kim smiles and tells her that she'll be with her in about five minutes. Principal Kim then turns and heads back into her office, leaving Tamika alone with Anthony.

"Hey," Tamika says.

"Hey."

Anthony wrings his hands nervously, opening and

closing his mouth as if he wants to say something else but can't quite find the words.

"You look . . . really . . . nice," he says finally.

Tamika looks down, takes in her khaki pencil skirt and fitted black polo, and looks back up, confused. Then, after remembering that Anthony has only ever seen her in basketball shorts, she smiles sheepishly. "Thank you."

A clumsy silence engulfs them. Anthony kicks at the ground but is slow to leave. As he lingers, Tamika attempts to calm the uneasiness between them.

"So why were you meeting with Principal Kim?" she asks carefully.

Anthony's awkward smile collapses, and Tamika immediately wishes she had said something else. Maybe she should have mentioned Hoop Group or asked about the football game that was on TV the night before. *He probably likes football, right?*

"It's a long story," Anthony says finally.

"Oh, yeah, right," Tamika says, waving a hand as if she can physically dismiss her question. "You don't have to tell me if you don't want to."

"No. It's not that I don't want to tell you . . ." Anthony takes a deep breath. "It's just that, uh, I need to go talk to my science teacher before class starts."

Tamika watches closely as Anthony grows shifty, suddenly unwilling to look her in the eyes. She smiles and says "okay," and as she watches Anthony walk away, she hopes that they really will have the chance to talk again.

A few minutes later, Tamika is seated across from Principal Kim, surrounded by pictures of the principal smiling with her husband and three kids. In one, they are skiing in Aspen; in another, they are snorkeling off the coast of Hawaii; in yet another, they are traipsing through Disney World's Epcot Center. Tamika is momentarily distracted by the image of Principal Kim's daughter smiling up into the face of her father, but when she hears the principal clear her throat, she is able to refocus and dive straight into her planned spiel.

Tamika tells Principal Kim that she grew up around basketball, that she is easily one of the most talented kids in the entire Hoop Group program. She also shares her achievements from Austinberg and explains that she dreams of following in the footsteps of Carolyn Peck, Dawn Staley, and Adia Barnes—that leading Hoop Group feels like a natural first step, however early it may be.

Principal Kim is nodding and smiling, and Tamika can't help but believe that her plan is working. She is thrilled to think that she'll be the new Coach Beck to carry Hoop Group into the future, but the letdown from Principal Kim is swift and merciless.

"The problem is not your basketball knowledge or your ability to coach the team from a basketball perspective," Principal Kim says. "The problem is that you're only in seventh grade. You'll have to have a permanent adult chaperone for the program to continue, and since the semester's already started, most of our teachers are already committed to whatever after-school activities they're going to do."

"What about Miss Turner?" Tamika says, grasping for any hope that may remain.

"Miss Turner is only staying on through the end of the week. I'm sorry, but she also has other commitments."

In an instant, Tamika feels as if the walls are closing in around her, as if her window of opportunity to play in Hoop Group—let alone coach it—is being shut before it ever fully opened. She worries that Principal Kim is going to tell her that Hoop Group will be canceled once the week is over, once Miss Turner goes back to whatever she's going back to, so without giving it a second thought, she blurts out: "Why can't you volunteer?"

Tamika girds herself in advance of the response that she is sure is coming. She was too forward, too forceful, and now she fully expects that Principal Kim will snuff out whatever little bit of life Hoop Group has remaining.

But Principal Kim actually pauses to consider Tamika's request. She hasn't said yes, but she also hasn't said no. And before she can, Tamika plays the only card she has left.

"Honestly, Principal Kim, I'm doing this for my dad," Tamika says, her voice cracking. "He's spent his whole life coaching us kids, and now that he can't, I think it's making everything worse."

For added impact, Tamika forces up the widest, brightest smile she can muster. Principal Kim doesn't need to know that she is still furious with her dad for dismissing her basketball interests and abilities. She doesn't need to know that, of all the people Tamika has told about her dreams to play, and later coach, women's basketball, her own father is the only one who's made it feel impossible.

Principal Kim doesn't need to know any of that

because, for the good of Hoop Group, Tamika is willing to keep her heartbreak to herself. In fact, for the good of Hoop Group, she is willing to lean in even further. "If I can show my dad how much he meant to me—to this school, to this community—by carrying on the Hoop Group legacy . . . I think it'll really help him stay motivated to, you know, stay healthy. To beat his Parkinson's."

As Principal Kim sits in silent thought, twirling her pen around and around in her fingers, Tamika steals another glance at the photos of a family so happy, so united. She feels her smile start to slip, but Principal Kim responds just in time.

"Fine," she says flatly. "I'll chaperone Hoop Group."

CHAPTER 10

THE CAFETERIA AIR IS HEAVY with the scent of sloppy joes and yellow sheet cake as Tamika navigates the maze of long rectangular tables. Her own home-made lunch, turkey and brie on a brioche roll, remains untouched. Now that Principal Kim is on board as Hoop Group's permanent chaperone, a full season is once again possible, and Tamika doesn't have time to eat. She's on a mission to lure kids back to the program and turn them into a team again.

Chris is holding court with three other former Hoop Groupers when Tamika strolls up to their table and takes a seat. "I just had a talk with Principal Kim," she says, her voice devoid of emotion. "Hoop Group is back on and official tryouts are in two days."

Chris places his bag of plain potato chips back on his tray and turns his body toward Tamika. "Who are you talking to?"

"I'm obviously talking to y'all," Tamika says as she waves her hand in a circular motion in front of the four boys.

"Nah. You can't be talking to us. We already got a team."

Tamika cocks her head to the side, as if the misunderstanding is simply the result of not hearing Chris properly. "What team?"

Chris smiles, his lips dripping with disdain. "Oh, you ain't heard? My pops started a new program. Down at the Y. It's called the Ballers, and it's the best basketball program in Lorain."

Tamika feels heat rising in her chest and stands up from the table.

"I hate to break it to you," Chris continues, "but Hoop Group is washed. Anybody who's worth anything is down with the Ballers." Chris looks at the boys gathered around him like pigeons angling for a single cube of bread. "Y'all feel me, right?"

There is a chorus of *yep*s and *fa sho*s, but Tamika can't hear any of it. The warmth has risen to her face, and her brain is furiously trying to salvage her own comeback from the wreckage of her Hoop Group hopes.

She opens her mouth, ready to annihilate Chris and his minions, but she is stunned when the words she hears next aren't hers. They're Anthony's.

"So anybody who's worth anything is playing with the Ballers?" he says, stepping up to the table and towering over a still-seated Chris. "Tell me why you on the team, then. 'Cause last time we saw you, you definitely didn't look like much of a *baller*."

Chris is on his feet now, too, smirking and posturing as his entourage looks on. Tamika takes note of the *ooooooh*s that trickle over from nearby tables as he steps up to Anthony, bold, like the six-inch height difference means nothing.

"I know you ain't talking, big boy," Chris says. "You the one who's ten feet tall and still can't make a layup."

This is enough to elicit a full-on uproar from Chris's table. His boys slap fives in praise of their fearless leader while Tamika watches as Anthony's face gathers into an angry scowl.

"I never said I was a baller; that's what you say about yourself," Anthony says. "It's just a shame Jayden ate you up so bad you had to run home and cry to your daddy about it."

Chris shrugs. "Yeah, okay." Then a pause. "But at least I *can* run home and cry to my daddy."

In an instant the cafeteria falls silent, even way across the room where the cheer squad had been engaged in a rather loud back-and-forth about an article in the new issue of *Sesi Magazine*. Everyone—*everyone*—is waiting for Anthony's next move.

Already, there were only a couple of feet separating the two boys, but Anthony closes them quickly, his eyes tight and focused.

"Still wanna be Floyd Mayweather, huh?" Chris says, refusing to back down. "Go ahead and hit me, then, so I can tell Principal Kim your li'l punishment ain't working." He shakes his head and turns to Tamika: "You might wanna tell your guard dog to back up, before y'all end up with only two players in Hoop Group."

In a flash, Tamika steps in between Chris and Anthony and, with all the strength she can muster, shoves Anthony away from Chris's table. "Everybody just *stop*!" she says.

This is the second time she's seen Chris push someone to the edge like this, and after seeing Anthony outside of Principal Kim's office, she is worried that Chris might have pushed Anthony a little too far.

Tamika leads Anthony to an empty table far from Chris and his cronies. Once they're out of earshot and Anthony's breathing has returned to normal, with softness in her heart and her eyes, she says, "What the heck is going on with you?"

That morning, when Anthony told Tamika he'd talk to her later, he hadn't imagined that later would come so soon—neither had he imagined that Chris King would try him like that in front of half the seventh grade. But life changes just like the cafeteria runs out of bacon during free breakfast—quickly and frequently—so with no other option, Anthony takes a deep breath and tells Tamika everything.

He tells her what happened at the end of last school year, how he'd asked if Tyson Rowley was going to finish his lunch, even though he didn't actually want Tyson's stupid bologna sandwich. Then Tyson gave it up, and somehow, the sandwich wasn't enough; it was just too easy. Anthony asked Tyson for his homework next, then his phone. All of it dropped in Anthony's lap with no resistance, no pushing or pulling, none of the drama he was used to at home.

It made Anthony snap. He hadn't meant to. Not really. He just wanted Tyson to tell him to stop, to put up even half of a fight. But he didn't. He wouldn't. Tyson just kept on giving in, so Anthony resorted to the only other thing he knew to do. He split Tyson's lip and sent Tyson to the hospital with a possible concussion.

When he finishes the story, Anthony says nothing about the shock on Tamika's face, how her cocoa-colored eyes are now wide and unblinking. Instead, he tells her about Principal Kim's commitment to working with kids who've been in trouble before—even when it seems like those kids have nothing left to work with. Principal Kim says that helping kids become well-functioning people outside of the classroom is just as important as teaching them math and science inside of it, so, in addition to making him join Hoop Group, she meets with Anthony twice a week to talk about whatever's on his mind.

"What do y'all talk about?" Tamika says.

Anthony sighs and rubs a large hand over his forehead.

"I don't know. Mostly my dad, I guess."

Lately, Anthony's dad has been drunk far more often than he's been sober. He comes stumbling home in the evening, sweaty and belligerent after he's stopped at some bar and spent money he doesn't have on liquor he doesn't need. It wasn't always like that, though. Back when Anthony's dad was a staff accountant at the local children's hospital, when it was his job to make sure families paid their kids' medical bills, he was home by 6:00 and spent most evenings cradling a bottle of Cherry Coke. He had a tendency to anger then, too, but his rage was always restrained, never reckless.

Then Anthony's dad got laid off, and not being able to pay his own family's bills seemed to break something inside of him. All at once, everything changed.

The arguments between Anthony's parents—about money, about Anthony, about the daytime drinking—grew increasingly violent until one day—one ugly, dreary day in the middle of January—Anthony's dad got so mad that he pushed Anthony's mom down a flight of stairs. She was paralyzed instantly.

The following weeks were a blur of police officers, case workers, and family therapists. Because Anthony's father said the fall was an accident and his mother agreed, no charges were pressed. But that still couldn't save their family from the chaos that consumed them. Anthony's little brother, Beans, was shipped off to live with an aunt in Atlanta, while Anthony stayed behind, pledging to protect his mother no matter what.

Anthony stops talking now and takes in air slowly through his mouth, willing his body to calm. Of all the terror and trauma, this is the part of the story that triggers him the most. Even though he's the one telling it, he never feels like the story belongs to him. If he's honest, his mother's fall and the never-ending fallout feel like someone else's nightmare, even if they both continue to haunt his every waking hour.

Anthony counts his breaths just like Principal Kim taught him to—*one-one-thousand, two-one-thousand, three-one-thousand*—then he continues.

For a while, Anthony tells Tamika, his dad was so overcome with regret and grief that the drinking stopped. But with his mom in a wheelchair and unable to work, the pressure on Anthony's dad soon began to snowball. He started working around the clock—collecting trash here, painting houses there—and doing whatever he could to keep the lights on and the fridge at least halfway full.

Thankfully, Anthony's dad is able to take care of the family's basic necessities, but there is little money left at the end of the month. For him, there's even less life.

Over the last six or seven months, Anthony's dad's frustration has been pooling, gathering like a slowly warming pot of water that is moments away from bubbling over. Now that the drinking has started back up again, so, too, have the outbursts. And now that Anthony's mom has lost all independence and ability to fight back, most of those outbursts are directed toward Anthony.

Principal Kim says that Anthony's dad is just disappointed in himself and his circumstances, that he feels helpless and unable to change things for the better. Anthony wants to believe her, but his instinct is to blame himself when his father lashes out. After all, his grades haven't been great, and he struggles to stay out of trouble. All of this just places more stress on his family, he believes, so he absorbs his father's rage and stuffs it deep within. There it festers until, as with any wound left unhealed, it gets infected and seeps out, rotten and stinking, for everyone to see.

When Anthony finally looks up, after talking for what feels like hours, he half expects Tamika to have run away. But there she remains, with care and empathy etched into her perfectly beautiful brown skin.

"I'm really sorry," Anthony says. "I didn't mean to talk so much. I'm sure you probably didn't want to hear—"

"No, I'm glad you told me," Tamika says, gently interrupting. "And I'm so sorry you have to deal with all that." Her lips spread into a smile. "I know it probably doesn't mean much since you're not really into basketball, but I am glad that you're in Hoop Group. Really. And this is going to be the best Hoop Group season ever. I promise."

In the next moment, the bell rings to signal the end of the lunch period, and Anthony watches as Tamika offers one last smile, throws her bag over shoulder, and rushes off down the hall. He watches as she blends in so effortlessly with the other middle schoolers, all the other kids whose lives must be ten times better than his. Anthony watches them, but he doesn't move. He doesn't move because he is frozen, weighted by the gravity of Tamika's judgment-free acceptance.

IT'S THE DAY OF Hoop Group tryouts, and Tamika is running late. She stayed past the final bell to talk to her pre-algebra teacher, and now she has to sprint to the gym. She arrives, huffing and puffing, not wanting to make a bad first impression with any newcomers. But when she hits the court and sees only Anthony and Dex sitting on the bleachers, her feet stop and her spirit drops.

"Good afternoon, Tamika," Principal Kim says from her chair in the corner of the gym. "It appears as though these two gentlemen are your only participants today."

Tamika doesn't understand. She just knew that after the cafeteria scene between Anthony and Chris, some of the kids would have shown up just to see what the new Hoop Group was all about. If nothing else, the dozens of signs Principal Kim let her post in the school's hallways should have led at least a handful of new kids to the gym.

Truthfully, Tamika had been holding out hope that some of Carter Middle's football and baseball players would show up. She knew she'd have to work overtime to get them up to speed and teach them some basketball basics, but she was willing to do that. At least they'd be athletic enough to pick the game up quickly.

Instead she was left with two of the least coordinated kids in the whole school.

Tamika plops down on one of the lower bleachers and buries her head in her hands. Sensing her disappointment, Principal Kim pulls her chair over and sits directly in front of the three kids.

"I'd like to do an exercise with you guys," Principal Kim says. "I want us to take a moment, close our eyes, and just listen. No one is going to be talking, so we won't be listening to each other. This is a moment to listen to ourselves, to really understand the issues that are weighing heavily on our hearts so that we can find the best, most authentic solutions."

Tamika looks first at Dex and Anthony, who are already lowering their heads and closing their eyes, and then back at Principal Kim. "This is a joke, right? Like, I don't understand what we're doing here. My heart's not saying anything, so I don't have anything to *listen* to."

"Now, Tamika," Principal Kim says calmly and with a smile, "we both know that's not true. I saw the look on your face when you walked into the gym. There's a lot going on inside of you, and I want you to take just a few minutes to tap into that."

Tamika rolls her eyes but closes them—reluctantly. Moments later, she hears music coming from what she assumes is Principal Kim's cell phone. Not long after that, she feels herself drawn in by lyrics like *There is no way you can't win / Just have the strength to begin, again* and *Though trouble's right beside you / There's nothing you can't do.*

Tamika doesn't know the song, but her body is instinctively rocking to the driving drum beat and the chorus of powerful voices.

Once the music ends and Principal Kim tells the kids to open their eyes again, Tamika feels equally emboldened and conflicted. Yes, her heart feels stretched toward endless possibility, but she is also firmly grounded in reality. And with everything seeming to go wrong—with basketball, with her dad—being optimistic seems nearly impossible.

"Now," Principal Kim says, her smile wider than ever. "I want you to tell me what the song meant to you and how you think it applies to your own life. Who wants to share first?"

Tamika looks over and is surprised to see Anthony raise his hand. "Um . . . so . . . I think everybody knows that I've been dealing with a lot of stuff at home, and . . . um . . . it is real hard to be positive about everything most of the time. Like, sometimes I just don't know if things will ever get better." Anthony looks up at Principal Kim, whose grinning face encourages him to keep talking.

"So . . . um . . . the song really meant a lot to me because I think it's saying that even if it seems like you can't win, that's not always the case. And, like, I really feel that way about Hoop Group. I obviously can't quit or anything, but I am glad I'm on this team. I mean . . . I know we don't technically *have* a team right now, but . . . I've learned a lot already, and being here has really helped me take my mind off of . . . other stuff."

Principal Kim is nodding so forcefully that Tamika

is sure her head is going to pop off her body like a broken bobblehead doll. And while she's certainly happy for Anthony's breakthrough, she's a little upset that her Hoop Group practice was hijacked by this impromptu group therapy session.

It appears as though she's the only one upset, however. Before she can shift the conversation to a new recruitment strategy, Dex raises his hand and jumps in.

"I know you're upset that more people didn't come," he says, turning to Tamika, "but that's okay. We just have to keep going, just like the song says. We can still make Hoop Group gr—"

With this, Tamika stands up, her eyes wild with exasperation. "Make Hoop Group what, Dex? We can't make Hoop Group anything without an actual *Hoop Group*, and we can't have a *Hoop Group* if we don't have players. I mean, y'all let that little song get y'all hype, but trust and believe: *thinking positive thoughts* isn't going to save this program." She stops and sighs. "Maybe Chris was right. Maybe this was just a waste of time."

"No!" Anthony says, Jumping from his own seat. "Chris was completely *wrong*, and you know that." He waits a beat, and then, with pleading in his voice, says,

"You told me this season would be the best Hoop Group season ever, and I believed you."

Anthony and Tamika exchange a brief glance before Dex jumps in. "Yes!" he says. "It *will* be the best! I know I'm not super fast or big, and I'm not really a good shooter, either, but I know a *lot* about the game. I probably know more than any other seventh grader in all of Lorain." He pauses, smiles at Tamika, adds, "Outside of you, of course."

"Oh, really?" Tamika says.

"Yeah. Really! Ask me anything! I mean, I can show you how to run a two-three zone when the other team—"

Tamika rolls her eyes and cuts him off. "The problem with a two-three zone is that you need five people. Two plus three is *five*, Dex. You got any advice on how to run a *three* zone? Or how to get us another two?"

Embarrassed, Dex drops his head. "I didn't mean to—"

"No," Anthony says to him, lightly pushing his right shoulder. "Don't apologize. There's nothing wrong with trying to come up with a plan. We can't give up on Hoop Group."

Silence falls over the trio, and Dex's eyes slide back and

forth between Anthony and Tamika. He hesitates, then hesitates some more. Finally, he says, "I have another idea. A good one."

"I'm listening," Tamika says.

Dex takes a deep breath and locks eyes with Tamika. "Okay. So. Hear me out. A lot of kids left because Coach Beck stepped down, right?"

"Yeah. So?"

"So . . . What if, as part of the program, we tell kids that they'll get access to weekly coaching and training with Coach Beck, even though he won't be leading the actual team?"

"Like an incentive for signing up?" Anthony says.

"Yeah. Exactly. I mean, he wouldn't really be coaching, but lots of kids would probably come if they knew they were going to get some one-on-one training with the same coach who developed Kendrick King."

Anthony nods. "That makes sense, but how are we supposed to get Coach Beck to agree to come back when none of us know him like that?"

Dex turns back toward Tamika and waits, as if passing the proverbial mic. She refuses to take it.

"Well," Dex says, pushing forward on his own. "Since

Coach Beck is Tamika's dad, maybe she could ask."

Tamika watches as surprise flickers across Anthony's face. Then she watches as it turns to something else, something like distrust.

It's not that she was trying to keep a secret from the other players; she just didn't want to deal with the pressure of coming into a new school *and* being the daughter of the most famous youth basketball coach in the entire state. Part of her wants to say this, to explain herself, but she doesn't.

"How did you know he's my dad?" she asks Dex instead.

Dex shrugs. "I found out by accident, really. I have a newspaper clipping of an article about an old Hoop Group championship. You must have been, like, two or three years old. I pulled it out last week, after Coach Beck stepped down, and I saw the name printed under the photo: Tamika Beck."

"Also," Dex adds, "your shooting form has Coach Beck written all over it."

Tamika ignores Principal Kim, who is laughing quietly under her breath. And while she acknowledges Dex's detective work, she also refuses to comment, let alone commit to such a ridiculous plan. She won't say as much to Dex or Anthony, but there's no way she's asking her dad for help. No way at all.

She'll just have to figure out another way to rebuild Hoop Group.

CHAPTER 12

DAYS PASS, and much to Dex's dismay, the possibility of Hoop Group having a real season is still a long shot. Tamika, Anthony, and Dex continue to show up in the gym every day at 3:00; Principal Kim continues to come, too—mostly just to watch them do three-man weaves up and down the court.

Still, Dex holds out hope that the situation will see a sudden shift, that they will walk into the gym on a normal Tuesday afternoon and see dozens of kids stretching and shooting, just like they were on the first day of school.

And in the interim, there is, well . . . *school.*

Dex, Chris, Anthony, and Jayden are sitting in their

Creative Writing class, finishing up their daily journal entries, when Ms. Cahill announces that she is splitting the class up into pairs to work on their writing projects. "Sometimes two heads are better than one," she says in her singsong way. "And sometimes our peers can see things in our writing that we can't see on our own. So when I match you with your partner, I encourage you to be open to sharing. Be vulnerable and transparent with your thoughts."

Dex is crushed by this latest turn of events. There are no tests in Creative Writing, so this assignment is going to comprise the majority of the semester's grade. That alone isn't cause for trouble, though. Dex is more left-brained than right, more technical than creative, but he is confident in his ability to score well in a writing class—*if* he can work alone. Academics aren't a team sport, and in Dex's experience, group projects only serve to ruin his grades.

Dex likes school, and he hasn't missed a day since Mrs. Cunningham's first-grade class at Laurel Tree Elementary. He's also never gotten a grade lower than an A on any report card. (There was Mr. Phillips's sixth-grade world history class, when Dex's grade hovered perilously close to an 89 percent all semester long, but a voluntary fifteen-page report on the Haitian Revolution against French colonial rule gave him the boost he needed.)

Like Jayden, Dex dreams of enrolling in Willow Brook Academy after graduating from Carter Middle School. Every year, he drops his address and mother's name into the contact form on Willow Brook's website to *Request More Information*, and every year he races to the mailbox to grab the most current copy of the prospective student brochure, the course catalog, the letter of greeting from Dr. Malcolm Shropshire.

Though Dr. Shropshire was the star point guard from Willow Brook's 1998 state championship basketball team, he's now better known for earning a PhD from Stanford University and coming back to serve as headmaster of his alma mater. Dex hopes to take a similar path. He doesn't want to go to Willow Brook to play sports. He wants to take the kinds of classes and participate in the types of extracurricular activities that will secure his own spot at Stanford, or some other elite college. He then plans to become a wealth manager for high-earning athletes. This'll put him as close to the NBA action as he could ever hope to get, and Dex is totally okay with that. He may not be good enough at basketball to become the next

Gary Payton, but he'll be good enough at his job to tell the guy who *is* the next Gary Payton how to invest his money.

While Ms. Cahill runs a finger over her class roster, Dex wonders who his partner is going to be. He looks to his left at Sierra, a mahogany-colored girl with waist-length box braids who transferred to Carter in the middle of last year and quickly established herself as one of the smartest kids in their grade. She's a know-it-all, and although she'd probably rip whatever idea he has to shreds, she'd at least be as committed to getting an A on the assignment as Dex is.

Next, he looks to his right at Anthony, who's hunched over his desk, pencil scribbling wildly across his paper. He's still writing in his journal, a task that Ms. Cahill requires at the beginning of every class. *This is an opportunity to take whatever is on your mind or heart and put it on the page,* she says. The students only have to produce one single-spaced page, but Anthony always writes three or four.

"Dexter," Ms. Cahill says, interrupting his thoughts, "you'll be working with Chris today."

Dex nods and slides into the desk next to Chris's. He is certainly relieved that he won't be forced to work with Anthony, but he's not sure what to make of Chris or his work ethic. Less than a minute later, Chris lets Dex know exactly where he stands.

"Look, man," he says, "I don't really feel like doing this right now."

Dex looks up at Ms. Cahill, who has announced that she'll start making rounds to check on everyone soon. "Uh, I don't think we really have a choice."

Chris reclines in his seat, stretching his legs long and crossing them at the ankles. "Go 'head and do what you gotta do. I'm just saying, for me, writing's not really my thing."

Dex feels his straight-A heart start to speed. "We're supposed to be working together. What are we gonna say when Ms. Cahill comes by?"

"We should probably act like we have something to talk about," Chris says nonchalantly. After a beat, he adds, "What about basketball? Didn't I see you on the first day of Hoop Group?"

Dex nods, and then, with the seed of an idea taking root in his gut, he pivots his focus from Creative Writing and decides to bust open the door of opportunity that has been cracked before him.

For the next twenty minutes, Dex talks up Hoop Group, telling Chris about Tamika's incredible coaching skills and how she's almost turned Anthony into a real-deal big man. Dex also tells him that Principal Kim is totally on board with Hoop Group having a season, if—and it's a *big* if—they can actually get enough kids to field a team.

"You should come back," Dex says. His eyes are steady and pleading, but of course, Chris just laughs.

"Y'all ain't Hoop Group. Y'all the Hoop Trio. And why would I come back to that when I'm already on a team?"

"Because . . . ," Dex says, readying for his big reveal, "if you come back, I'll help you with your assignment for this class."

The smile is gone from Chris's face in an instant. "Oh yeah? How you gon' help me?"

"You said writing's not your thing, right?"

"Yeah."

"So I'll help you with whatever you need."

Chris is doubtful but also aware that his options are limited. "For real?" he says.

Dex smiles. "For real."

That afternoon, after the shock of Chris's arrival at Hoop Group practice begins to dissipate—and after Anthony and Chris agree to squash their earlier cafeteria beef—Tamika decides to take advantage of the extra body by staging another game of two-on-two. This time, it's Chris and Dex versus her and Anthony.

They play two games. Afterward, with sweat dripping into his eyes, blurring his vision, Chris looks up at the gym's clock: 4:46. He has only a few minutes before he'll have to hop on his bike, fly over to the Lorain Y, and settle back into his role as the heir to the Kings' throne.

When he agreed to Dex's deal, Chris's expectations for Hoop Group were low. Very low. Yet he quickly discovered that the team actually has promise (if three people can be considered a team, that is).

To be clear, the Hoop Groupers are far from *good*. Anthony still looks lost on the court, and he would be called for countless lane violations in a real game. Dex, meanwhile, can barely get the ball to the rim when he shoots. But they're not *bad*, either. There's a budding sense of togetherness that wasn't there on the first day of the season. On top of that, Chris feels comfortable around them, almost like he can actually be himself.

"So," Tamika says between gulps of Gatorade, "did you quit the Ballers or what?"

Chris nearly chokes on his own drink. "Of course I didn't quit. Why would I quit?" He pauses, clears his throat. "I just . . . worked something else out."

Chris doesn't tell the Hoop Groupers this, but since the Ballers practices don't start until 4:00, he's already figured that even if he stays for most of the Hoop Group practice, he can still get to the Ballers right around 5:00. To account for the missing hour, he'll tell his father that he has to stay after school for extra help, that he'll get to practice as soon as he can. His dad will be surprised, but Chris doesn't expect much pushback.

"Does that mean you're coming back for real, then?" Tamika says as she lifts an eyebrow in disbelief.

"I don't know," Chris says after a couple seconds of thought. "I mean, what's even the point? Even if I came every day, y'all still don't have a team without five people."

"Yeah, well, we're working on that," Tamika snaps.

Chris snorts a laugh. He knows full well no one is coming to Hoop Group anymore. "Okay. Tell me the plan, then."

"Just trust me, okay?" Tamika says with her eyes on the floor and the toe of her sneaker kicking against the sideline paint. "We're working on it."

"Yeah. Well. I'll believe it when I see it."

"And when you see it," Dex cuts in, "when you see that we have a full team, will you come back for real?"

Chris hesitates. He'd never expected this to turn into anything; he was only there because of the deal he made with Dex.

"Yeah," Tamika adds, her eyes meeting Chris's. "If we have a 'real' team, with four other people, will you come back then?"

Chris's mind is racing, searching for an out. "How 'bout this," he says, finally. "If you can get Jayden to come back to Hoop Group, I'll come back, too."

"Wait," Anthony says. "Isn't Jayden already on the Ballers?"

Dex and Tamika nod with agreed confusion. Jayden hadn't come back to Hoop Practice since the day he walked out. No one dared to consider that he wasn't playing basketball at all.

Chris shakes his head emphatically. "Nah. Jayden definitely ain't a Baller."

Suddenly, there is a loud clap from Dex, as he considers the possibility that Hoop Group might become a real team after all. "This is great!" he says. "If Jayden isn't on the Ballers, I'm *sure* we can get him to come back!"

Chris sneers at Dex's enthusiasm, at how his glass is always half-full. Chris doesn't expect them to convince Jayden to come back any more than he expects his father to let him leave the Ballers. But there's Tamika, jumping in and signing on to Dex's plan. "Okay, it's a deal," she says. "We'll get Jayden to join and then you'll come back, too!"

Chris takes a long swig of his water before saying, simply, "Maybe." While he wants to make sure he's not committing to anything, he knows he doesn't want to rule anything out, either. And that fact surprises him more than he'd ever let on.

CHAPTER 13

IT'S ALMOST 3:30 when Jayden first sets foot in the main gym at the Lorain Y. He expected to be alone for a while, to have time to run the court, to warm up before warm-ups. But even with a full half an hour remaining before practice is set to begin, there are already a couple dozen kids hanging around the gym—far more than one team could possibly hold.

From the corner near the entrance, Jayden watches, anxious. With every swish of a net and call for the ball, something inside him aches. On this day, he's a visitor in someone else's house.

Jayden is still watching the activity on the court when,

at 4:00 on the dot, Cam King walks to the center of the floor to start practice. At 6'3" and 215, Cam is a smaller, flabbier version of his younger brother, Kendrick. Still, his giant-sized persona easily spreads to every inch of the gym. Cam's gait is relaxed but determined; when he talks, his words are laced with charisma and authority. And as he watches, Jayden understands why Chris is, well, *Chris.*

After stretching and conditioning drills, Cam forms two teams of five kids each. The goal is to stage a scrimmage, and Jayden can't help but wonder why Cam's not running two games at the same time. After Cam's A and B squads are picked, there are at least fifteen kids still sitting on the bench.

Once Cam begins calling plays from the sidelines and subbing kids in and out, Jayden quickly realizes that something else is off, too. At least four of the really good kids from last year's Hoop Group—including Tyshaun Thompson, last season's second-leading scorer—are barely playing. Meanwhile, kids who are struggling to dribble up and down the court are allowed to rack up crazy minutes. It doesn't make sense, especially if Cam is trying to run a program as competitive as Hoop Group.

Minutes later, with the first game in the books, Cam

calls for a ten-minute break and instructs everyone to grab water. He then looks over at Jayden and greets him with a wide grin. Jayden had intended to sit back and remain unseen, but as the scrimmage wore on and the play got more intense, Jayden felt himself being sucked into the action, his body easing closer and closer to the floor. Now he's standing directly across from the bench as Cam glides over.

"What's good, Jayden?" Cam says, dapping him up. "Wasn't expecting you to come through, but I ain't mad about it at all."

Jayden smiles nervously. "Uh. Thanks, I guess? I mean, I just wanted to come see what y'all were all about—"

"It's all good," Cam says, punching Jayden's arm playfully. "Be easy; it's just basketball."

Another smile. "Okay."

"I'm Cam King, by the way. Chris's dad."

"I know," Jayden says.

"Cool. Well, let me tell you a little bit about myself and what I'm trying to build with the Ballers."

Cam explains that he used to hoop, that he started for the Carter High varsity team when he was just a sophomore. Jayden already knew all of that; he also knew that

Cam was never as good as Kendrick, that Carter High was maybe the fifth-best program in the city, well below Willow Brook in the city-wide standings. Jayden doesn't say this, of course. He just smiles and nods.

"You know, the Ballers could really use a guy like you," Cam says.

Suddenly uncomfortable, Jayden glances over at the bench where Tyshaun is seated and dribbling a ball behind his legs.

As if sensing his thoughts, Cam quickly adds, "We're all about development here, and we want everyone to have a solid shot at playing basketball." He then slides in front of Jayden, blocking his view of the court. "But trust me, Jayden: if *you* join the Ballers, you'd be the star, most def."

Jayden wonders where Chris fits into the equation, but before he can say anything else—before he can even ask why Chris isn't at practice that day—Cam makes one final plea: "Look. Since we're already a few weeks into the season, here's what I can do: I'mma knock ten dollars off the registration fee just for you. A hundred and ninety dollars instead of two hundred. You can't beat it, and you're the only one I'm giving this offer to."

Jayden might struggle to remember dates and names

in American history, but math has never been a problem. It takes him only a couple of seconds to calculate that Chris's "big" discount is a measly 5 percent. But Cam's enthusiasm is undeniable, and he is fawning over Jayden, begging him to join. It feels so good to be wanted, even if the whole situation feels a little . . . shady.

"Thanks, Mr. King, but—"

"Please. Call me Coach Cam."

"Okay, Coach Cam," Jayden says. "Thanks for the offer. I really appreciate it. I just need to talk to my mom about it before I can say yes."

Cam waves a hand. "Of course. Just keep me posted and let me know if you have any questions or want me to holla at your mom for you. I'm here whenever, and I'm happy to tell her more about the program."

Jayden thanks Cam again and turns to leave. As he walks out of the gym, he thinks back to the conversation with Roddy on the Blocks, how it's his responsibility to make his dreams come. Jayden definitely has some unanswered questions about the Ballers, but his conversation with Cam still feels like a sure sign that the universe is laying out a special path, just for him. Getting the entrance fee will be a stretch, even with the (tiny) discount, but he's sure his mom will understand.

This is the belief that Jayden carries across town—past the boarded-up businesses, the dilapidated houses, the fathers begging for diaper money at the busiest intersections—and all the way back to Marsh and Seventeenth.

Unfortunately, as soon as Jayden gets home, as soon as he crosses the threshold into Grams's kitchen with the sweet, sweet corn bread baking in the oven and a giant pot of oxtail stew doing its thing on the stovetop, reality levels him with a devastating blow.

"I just don't understand," Grams says for the twelfth time in as many minutes. "You did every single thing that man asked you to do. And he just gon' fire you like that? Like you ain't got a son to feed?"

The feeling of dozens of needles tracing prickly lines up and down his spine forces Jayden straight up in his seat. It's bad enough that his mother just lost her job; now Jayden feels like he's making the problem even worse.

"I don't know, Mama," Jayden's mother says. "I just . . . I just don't know. He said something about needing to cut back on expenses, and——"

"Yeah, but you said you were the only assistant who got let go."

Jayden's mother sighs heavily. For four years she's been frustrated and *under*employed; now she's angry and worried and, most significantly, *un*employed. "That's what Layla in HR told me, but who knows, really," she says. "She's just an assistant herself, but it ain't no telling what's going on down there."

Grams *hmph*s as she tugs on her favorite oven mitt, the one with the yellow flowers, and pulls the corn bread from the oven. "I'mma tell you what's going on. That man done lost every bit of his mind."

"Mama."

"What, Sherice? What you want me to say? That food don't cost money? That bills ain't gotta be paid? That folk don't have to do right by other folk? Well, I ain't gon' say none of that, 'cause that would be a lie. And I ain't in the business of telling no lies."

An hour later, Jayden is lying across his bed and flipping through the latest issue of *Sports Illustrated Kids* when his mother comes in, her shoulders drooping under an impossibly heavy load.

"I don't want you to worry, Jayden," she says. "Everything's going to be fine. I'll make some calls tomorrow, and Grams is gonna look around, too."

Jayden lifts his eyes to his mother's, to the same expressive, deep brown, and now-tear-filled eyes as his own. Jayden's mother had only one year of law school left when she had to drop out to take care of Jayden, and by the time he was old enough for day care, it didn't matter that she had been in the top ten in her class. By then, there were too many bills to pay and too many responsibilities to even think of going back to school full-time.

Working for Boseman and Baxter after Greymont closed was supposed to be a pit stop en route to finishing her law degree. But the work kept getting harder and the days longer, and his mom just got more and more tired. . . .

Now, even the money that was never enough is gone, evaporated like a double-digit Celtics' deficit with Bill Russell on the floor. Still, Jayden appreciates his mother's optimism. He knows that any lawyer would be lucky to have her. But he's also scared of how long it will take her to find another gig—and what will happen to their family in the interim.

As for Grams, Jayden knows that job options are slim for a woman in her sixties who can't stand on her feet all day. Grams is a former high school English teacher, and Jayden overheard her telling his mom that she might consider substitute teaching for a while. The only problem is that subbing is sporadic—you never know when you'll get a call—and the Carr household needs money they can count on.

It seems to Jayden that his family is down to its last shot with only seconds on the clock. This is the elimination game, the contest that will determine whether they get to play on or get sent packing. It's clutch time, and if Jayden is going to prove that he deserves the ball when the game is on the line, this is the time to do it. Right now.

All he needs is a plan.

CHAPTER 14

"A GAME? WE'RE NOT READY for an actual game!" Dex's brow furrows above his glasses as his hands flail wildly in the air. "We don't even have enough people for a team!"

"I know that," Tamika says calmly. "That's why I told my cousin to only bring four of their players."

Dex's breathing evens, but only slightly. "I don't know, Tamika. I still don't think we're ready. We haven't even learned any plays. Personally, I don't feel—"

"Look," Tamika says, cutting him off, "we're never gonna *feel* ready until we have a reason to *get* ready. The Fall Invitational is around the corner. If we want to compete, we have to take this seriously. What happened to us being *optimistic*?"

Dex nods, but his face is still crumpled with concern. Nearby, Chris and Anthony only shrug. Anthony needs minimal convincing from Tamika to do just about anything. As for Chris? He's simply there to hold up his end of the deal with Dex so he can pass Creative Writing.

"I really think we'll be fine," Tamika adds. "Like, for real, everybody on my cousin's team is literally ten years old."

This should have brought Dex a moment of relief, but as soon as Tamika finishes speaking, the 10U Lorain Lady Legion comes busting through the gym doors. The girls may be ten-and-under, but Dex can't help but notice that they're all taller, and likely stronger, than he is.

There's a period of awkward hellos and competitive sizing up before Principal Kim takes her position as the referee. Minutes later, the game begins.

During the first couple of minutes of play, Tamika's prophecy appears to be accurate. Chris makes a couple of easy layups on fast breaks, and Tamika hits a couple of mid-range jumpers to keep the score close early on. At the same time, Anthony is displaying Rodman-like presence on D, shutting down the paint with relative efficiency, while Dex does a pretty good job not turning the ball over. It's a minor achievement but an important one, especially considering Dex's skill level just a few weeks before.

Unfortunately, as the game wears on, Hoop Group's collective effort just isn't enough. Like the Tin Man without a heart or Phil Jackson without a triangle, the Hoop Groupers are incomplete. They're a jumble of parts without the glue to hold them together.

By the beginning of the second half, the Lady Legion has fully adjusted their defense, double-teaming Tamika and forcing Hoop Group into a slower, half-court offense. Eventually, the shots stop falling, and without the ability to create momentum, a Hoop Group defeat becomes inevitable.

Once the game has ended and the fifth graders head back out the double doors, slapping fives and shouting praise, Dex's heart goes hollow with envy. He wants that kind of chemistry for Hoop Group, but at this rate, they'll be lucky to just get a fifth player. As practice ends, the Hoop Groupers gather on the bleachers to commiserate.

"What are we gonna do now?" Dex says, his eyes fixed on a hard, dry wad of gum stuck to the bleacher below him.

"Yeah," Anthony says, chiming in. "It's not a good look to lose to a bunch of ten-year-olds."

Tamika's eyes jump from Dex to Anthony. "Are y'all serious right now?" she says. "I can't believe y'all are talking like this. Maybe we lost, but at least we look like a team. That's more than I could say for us last week." She turns her attention to Anthony specifically. "Anthony, you're moving your feet so well and actually sliding on defense now. Once you learn to keep your arms straight up instead of hacking the shooter, nobody's going to be able to score on you."

Dex watches as Anthony, blushing, drops his head.

"And you, Dex," Tamika continues, "we're still working on your shot, but your ball handling is a lot better. You're protecting the ball when you dribble, and on defense, you're understanding how to force the guards to go to their nondominant side."

Tamika then turns to Chris, but before she can say anything, he holds a hand up to stop her.

"I don't need you to critique my game," Chris says. "I know I can hoop."

Tamika rolls her eyes.

"I'm just saying, though. It really doesn't matter how well anybody's playing. This whole thing is still a waste of time."

"Excuse me?" Tamika says.

"If you're trying to have a basketball team with four people, you're wasting your time. Y'all might be cool with that, but I'm not. I'm running back and forth between here and the Y, trying to make Hoop Group and the Ballers work, all 'cause y'all said this was gonna be a real team."

Tamika rolls her eyes again.

"Are you even still trying to find somebody else?"

All at once three sets of eyes turn toward Tamika, searching for answers.

"What about Jayden?" Chris says. "I thought y'all said y'all could get him to come back."

Tamika fidgets, pulling on a stray curl near her ear. Finally, without a trace of confidence, she says, "He'll be here. Jayden's been . . . busy, but he'll be here soon."

While the Hoop Groupers were trying to hold court against the Lady Legion, Jayden was in the midst of his own battle: trying to find a job.

As he was getting ready for bed the night before, Jayden told his mother that he wanted to help out, that he was going to figure out a way to earn some money while she looked for her next gig. Jayden expected his mother to be proud that he was stepping up as the man of the house, to maybe even reward him with a hug and a kiss. He got neither. Instead, Jayden's mother broke down in tears and ran from his room.

Moments later, Grams appeared with a glass of chocolate milk for Jayden and a mug of tea for herself. He could smell the lavender as soon as she hit the door.

Grams sat on the edge of Jayden's bed and muttered a prayer to Jesus under her breath; then she told him what she thought about his plan.

It is not your responsibility to earn money for this family, she'd said. *We're the adults, so that's our job. Right now you need to focus on being a kid and doing well in school . . . and playing basketball at Willow Brook Academy if that's what you really want to do. Focus on the things that are important to you and let your mom and me take care of the rest.*

Besides, Grams added before taking his empty glass and sending Jayden to the bathroom to brush his teeth, *you're too young to get a job anyway.*

Once Grams finished, Jayden could see why his mom had been upset enough to cry. He hadn't considered the shame she must have felt when her twelve-year-old son offered to get a job because she wasn't bringing in any money. Ultimately, though, neither Grams's nor his mother's feelings could keep Jayden from doing what he felt he must.

As Grams's eyelids grew heavy from her Sleepytime Tea, Jayden told her that he understood, that he was going to focus on school and basketball. But then, as soon as she left and Jayden found himself alone in the dark with only his thoughts to keep him company, he began piecing together a strategy.

Now, just an hour into his search for work—just sixty minutes of walking up and down the streets of Lorain's business district—Jayden has realized that Grams was right about at least one thing: He hasn't found a single business interested in hiring a twelve-year-old. Jayden had been turned away by a pet store, a fast-food chain, and a dry cleaner. His last-ditch effort was Slice, the local pizza joint just a few blocks from Carter Middle.

"Hi," Jayden says to the ponytailed teenager at the hostess stand. "I'm Jayden, and I was wondering if y'all were hiring for any extra help." He pauses briefly before pushing the rest of his words out back-to-back, in rapid succession: "I know I'm young, but I can clean tables or bathrooms, I can do whatever. I just really, really, *really* need the work."

Jayden lowers his head and, with his eyes, traces the diamond pattern on the tile beneath his feet. He braces himself for what he knows will happen next, the moment when the hostess will tell him that she's sorry but they can't hire him, that he should come back when he's sixteen.

"Nice to meet you, Jayden, I'm Lillian," he hears instead.

"Nice to meet you," Jayden says as he lifts his eyes.

Lillian smiles. "I've been working here since I was thirteen, so I get it. I'm not sure if my boss is hiring right now, but he's really cool. I'm sure he'd be happy to talk to you either way."

"Great," Jayden says, still surprised. "Thank you."

Lillian offers another reassuring smile. "If you wait here, I'll run and get him."

Jayden thanks Lillian again and waits patiently while she disappears into the kitchen at the back of the restaurant. A few minutes later, Jayden sees Roddy walking toward him in a black apron with the Slice logo on the front.

"What up, Jayden," Roddy says, smiling as he reaches him. "Lillian told me you're looking for work?"

Jayden shifts his weight. "Yeah, I am. But . . . are you the manager?"

Roddy chuckles and strokes his goatee. "Nah, man. I'm not the manager. I'm the owner."

Roddy and Jayden take a seat at an empty booth near the kitchen entrance while Jayden tells Roddy all about his family situation. He tells him that his mom lost her job, that even though she and his grandmother are looking for work, they need money for the mortgage and utilities right now.

"I'm sorry to hear that," Roddy says, "but I'm glad you

came and asked for help." He pauses, takes a look around the restaurant as if taking inventory of his needs. "I can't let you wait tables—it's against the law at your age—but I tell you what. If you can keep the tables clean, make sure the trash gets taken out regularly, and help wash dishes during busy shifts, you got yourself a job."

Jayden doesn't ask when he can start; he doesn't even ask how much he's going to make. He's already up from the table, shaking Roddy's hand and grinning from ear to ear. "Thank you *so* much, Roddy!" he says. "I promise to be the best dish washer and trash taker-outer you've ever hired!"

"I'mma hold you to that," Roddy says, laughing, "but before you go, I got one more question for you." Seconds pass and the smile that had just creased the corners of his eyes is now gone. "What about basketball?"

Slowly, Jayden slinks back into the booth, and the faux-leather covering the bench squeaks beneath him. "I don't know," he says after a while. "I haven't really thought about it."

"You haven't thought about basketball?"

"No." Jayden shakes his head. "That's not what I mean."

Truthfully, there is no need to ask Jayden whether he's

thought about basketball, whether he's considered how long he'll have to step away from the game he's loved nearly all his life. Of course he's thought about it. It's all he ever thinks about.

But there is also this: Jayden doesn't just hoop out of the love for the game. He hoops to take care of his mom, to give her everything she's never had and all she's ever deserved. This is the plan after Willow Brook, after college, after being selected as a lottery pick during the NBA draft on a sticky June night. At least that *was* the plan. That was the plan before his mother's jerk of a boss fired her and now refuses to pay out the overtime she'd racked up.

Now Jayden can't wait. His mom needs help *today*, and he has no choice but to step up.

"I'mma just go back to the Blocks, I guess," Jayden tells Roddy. "Early mornings, before school. I'mma just keep working and training on my own. I'm not giving up. Promise."

CHAPTER 15

"I HAVEN'T GOTTEN VERY FAR on the first draft, but I'll show you what I have," Dex says to Anthony right after Ms. Cahill splits the class into their new pairs, which was right after she told them that they're going to be working with a different partner every week so they can *experience the beauty of different perspectives.*

Anthony doesn't mind being partnered with Dex—at least he knows him and feels comfortable around him— but he can't imagine doing much of anything today, not after the morning he just had.

"So," Dex says as he pulls a sheet of notebook paper from his binder, "I'm writing an essay on the 1991–92

Cleveland Cavaliers and their upset of the Boston Celtics in the Eastern Conference Semifinals. Basically, they won because most of the team was able to stay healthy that year, so I wanna make the argument that a sports team's nutrition and medical staff is just as important as its scouts and coaches."

Anthony is barely listening. His mind is swimming, thoughts swirling.

"I can show you my outline, since I've already finished that," Dex continues. "Then I'll just read whatever you have."

"I ain't got nothing," Anthony says.

Dex studies Anthony's face, then glances down at Anthony's notebook, the one he was writing in at the beginning of class, the one he writes in every class . . . the one he spent hours writing in the night before.

Anthony had come home from Hoop Group buzzing, floating from spending another afternoon with Tamika. They never talk much at practice, especially not about anything other than basketball, but just being around her makes Anthony feel . . . different. Like maybe, *hopefully*, not everything in his life is terrible.

With no one to talk to about his feelings—about

Tamika or basketball or anything else—Anthony took to his writing, to the composition notebooks that have been his loyal companions for as long as he can remember. The words flowed like they always do, his deepest emotions and most private thoughts pouring onto the lined pages like water from a neighborhood fire hydrant that's been pried open on the hottest summer day.

For hours, Anthony sat at the rickety table in their small kitchen and wrote and wrote and wrote. He was still writing when his mother joined him, poking at the roast beef in the slow cooker to see if it was tender. He was still writing when she fixed their plates of meat and vegetables, the potatoes, carrots, and celery butter-soft and covered in jus. Anthony grabbed a couple of pieces of wheat bread and piled everything else on top, folding his dinner into a sandwich that allowed him to keep writing while he ate.

His mom never said a word, just chewed her own food in silence, her eyes fixed on the clock over the stove. As soon as she was done, she slid her plate into the sink and wheeled herself to her bedroom, locking the door closed behind her.

By the time his father showed up, spent and heavy

from the day, Anthony had retreated to his room as well. He'd planned to start writing again once he got there, but he took one look at his backpack filled with notebooks and syllabi and froze. All he could think about was his Creative Writing class and how, the next day, he'd have to share his work with someone else. Anthony knew that he wanted to write a collection of poems for his assignment, but that was as far as he'd gotten. Night after night, he'd prepare to work on his poems, but hours later, the page would still be as blank as it was when he started.

It was the fear of people reading his work that got him, the panic that comes from loving Langston Hughes and Gwendolyn Brooks and believing, deep down, that he could never measure up. How *could* Anthony ever compete with Hughes or Brooks or Giovanni or Sanchez. How could he hang with someone like Derek Walcott, who published his first poem when he was just fourteen? Deep down, Anthony knew he couldn't. He couldn't even finish a stupid class assignment.

But when the house grew quiet save for his father's snoring, Anthony sat down with his notebook and decided to start writing again. The words were still raw, but they were his. No one could ever take that from him, and for that alone, Anthony was proud. He was so proud that as he climbed into his bed that night, he was actually looking forward to the next day's Creative Writing class.

The expectancy spilled over into the next morning, too, buoying Anthony as he got dressed and packed his books, as he poured a bowl of cereal and threw a Ziploc bag full of Doritos into his bag. His anticipation was only interrupted when Anthony heard his father—saw him, actually—come crashing into the kitchen. His eyes were bloodshot, his temples pulsing, his body leaning just slightly off-kilter. "You woke me," he growled.

Anthony apologized and said that he'd tried to get ready for school as quietly as possible, but his pleas went unheard. The next moments were a loud and violent blur, his father's fury shattering any remaining optimism.

Now Anthony's back in Ms. Cahill's class, and while Dex is rambling on about some long-retired hoops stars, Anthony is both struggling to forget and determined to not let anyone read his words.

"I need to go to the bathroom," Anthony tells Dex. "I'll be back in a minute."

In his rush to escape Ms. Cahill's class, Anthony left his notebook on his desk, wide-open and vulnerable. It was a rookie mistake, and one that he'd soon be forced to reckon with.

For Dex's part, it's not like he really *meant* to snoop. He was just . . . curious.

Dex isn't sure what he expects to find when he slides Anthony's notebook over to his desk and begins fingering through the most recently written pages. He certainly isn't expecting a poem, and definitely not a poem written with such grace and sincerity. A love poem at that. It's still rough—Dex can see where Anthony has written and rewritten some lines multiple times—but it's good. Really good.

By the time Anthony walks back into the classroom, Dex has all but forgotten whose work he's reading. He's too taken by its power and the vivid emotion reflected on the pages. Dex looks up just in time to see Anthony coming toward him, and without thinking, Dex smiles. He's about to tell Anthony how talented he is, how much he loves his writing. But before he can get a word out, Dex is pressed against the wall, scrawny legs dangling, with Anthony's massive hands around his neck.

Fifteen minutes later, after Ms. Cahill pried them apart and hustled them down the hall, Anthony and Dex are sitting side by side in Principal Kim's office.

"I am really disappointed in you, Anthony," Principal Kim says, her hands clasped tightly atop her desk. "Actually, I'm more than disappointed. I'm angry and I'm frustrated, because I'm getting the sense that you're wasting my time. Is that your goal, Anthony? Are you trying to waste my time?"

"No ma'am."

"Well you're certainly disrespecting the other students and the safe learning environment my administration and I are trying to maintain for them."

A few feet away, Dex is on edge, waiting for the rebuke he's sure is coming his way next, but at every turn, Principal Kim continues to address Anthony. Being caught in Anthony's wrath was no fun at all, but Dex still can't help but feel bad—and somewhat guilty—about the verbal lashing Anthony's receiving.

"Perhaps Hoop Group wasn't the best fit for you," she says next. "It seems to me that you need something more structured that can better address your needs." She pulls a slip of paper from the top of her monogrammed notepad and starts scribbling. "I'm going to have a talk with your counselor about placing you somewhere else after school—"

"Excuse me," Dex cuts in, suddenly aware of the potential outcome of this meeting. "I'm sorry for interrupting, but is it okay if I say something?"

Dex ignores Anthony's stare and waits for Principal Kim's approval. Once she nods, he begins.

"I know that Anthony has been in trouble before, but this time wasn't his fault—at all."

"What do you mean?" Principal Kim says, narrowing her eyes.

Dex takes a deep breath. "So . . . we're partners in Creative Writing and we were supposed to be sharing what we've written so far on our class assignments. The project is kind of a big deal, like half our grade or something, but Anthony said he didn't have anything."

Dex pauses just long enough to briefly cut his eyes at Anthony, who's now staring at his hands. "The thing is," Dex continues, "Anthony is always writing. Like, *always*. So when he got up to go to the bathroom, I decided to take a quick look at his notebook."

"Without his permission?"

"Right," Dex says, quietly. "I didn't ask Anthony for permission."

"Well, Dexter, while I do appreciate your honesty and willingness to take responsibility for the altercation, Anthony's reaction was not a suitable response to your action. Do you understand that?"

"Yes, ma'am."

"Good. Now, as I was saying—"

"Excuse me," Dex says as he slowly lifts his right arm into the air. "Is it okay if I say one more thing?"

Frustrated, Principal Kim sighs and motions with her hand for Dex to continue.

"Listen, I know I was wrong, and I know Anthony was wrong. But you can't kick him out of Hoop Group. I mean, of course you *can* kick him out, but I'm just saying that I don't think you should."

"Really?" Principal Kim says. "And why is that?"

"Well, we really need him, for starters. Also, Anthony has the potential to be a really, really good basketball player. That's if he wants to be, I mean." Dex steals another glance at his teammate. "He's already a great writer, and I know it's not my place, but I think you really should read his stuff."

Finally, Principal Kim turns her attention back to Anthony. "Well, may I at least see the notebook in question?"

Without a word, Anthony reaches into his backpack, retrieves the notebook, and hands it to Principal Kim. As he does, Dex notices that Anthony's arm is shaking uncontrollably, and he is sweating profusely, too. Only then does Dex realize that he may have made the same mistake twice. First, he read Anthony's writing without Anthony's consent; now he's opened the door for Principal Kim to do the same.

Anthony's eyes are focused on his hands, but Dex watches as Principal Kim reads silently, as the hard frown on her lips begins to soften.

"This is indeed good work," she says when she looks up at Anthony again. "Very, very good work. But I still don't know that it has any bearing on what happened in Ms. Cahill's class. Your behavior was completely unacceptable, Anthony, and this isn't the first time you've exhibited unacceptable behavior."

Principal Kim waits a beat, then says, "Perhaps you'd like to explain to me, in *your* words, why you should be allowed to remain in Hoop Group."

Anthony's mind is racing fast, too fast for logical, rational thought. He wants to say that he doesn't care about Hoop Group, that protecting his property from nosy kids like Dex is far more important than some wack after-school basketball program that doesn't even have enough kids to make a real team.

But he doesn't say that.

"I want to stay in Hoop Group because I like being on the team," he says instead. "I'm not great, but I'm getting better and starting to actually like basketball. Plus, Tamika and Dex are, like, the only friends I have, I guess." This time Anthony glances over at Dex. "I was upset about him reading my notebook, so I overreacted. But if you give me another chance, it won't happen again."

Silent tension settles over the room like an August heat wave. It is thick, smothering, and unrelenting.

Finally, Principal Kim gets up from her seat and opens the door of her office, signaling to the boys that it's time for them to leave. "Okay, Anthony," she says sternly. "I will give you one last chance with Hoop Group. But when I say this is your last chance, I mean it."

Once Anthony and Dex are out of earshot and eyesight of Principal Kim, Dex clears his throat to get Anthony's attention. "Look, Anthony. I know I said this already, but—"

"If you've said it before, you don't need to say it again," Anthony says, keeping his eyes straight ahead.

"Yeah, I know, but I want to."

"Well, I don't want you to."

"I just wanna say that—"

Anthony steps directly in front of Dex, forcing him to stop walking. "It's over, okay? You don't have to apologize anymore. In fact, I don't want you to say anything about this ever again. Not to me, or anyone else. You got that?"

At first, Dex is shaken, maybe even a little frightened, but then something changes. His skinny arms flex tight and he squares up to Anthony as best he can. "You can't come at me like this just because I wanted to apologize," Dex says. "I read your notebook and you got upset, and I feel bad about that. So I can apologize for it, and you can accept my apology, okay? I'm not your freakin' enemy. I'm on your team, remember?"

Once he's finished, Dex stands, chest out, fully ready to be pounded into the ground. But to his surprise, Anthony nods and says simply, "Okay."

"Okay?" Dex asks.

Anthony nods, says it again. "Okay."

"So . . . I guess we should head to practice now?"

"Yeah," Anthony says. "I guess we probably should."

CHAPTER 16

CHRIS IS HEADING TO THE GYM, turning the corner near the Carter Middle School library, when he spots Jayden pulling a bag of Chex Mix from a vending machine. Chris had planned to talk to him sometime after Creative Writing, but with all the focus on Dex and Anthony's drama, Jayden had slipped out of Ms. Cahill's class before Chris had a chance to stop him.

"What up," Chris says as he angles his body against the vending machine.

"'Sup," Jayden says.

"Chillin'. On my way to Hoop Group. What about you?"

Jayden's eyes shift as he searches for a response. "I, uh, have some errands to run for my mom."

"That's cool," Chris says, though he's not at all convinced. "I guess I'll let you go, then, but, uh, I been meaning to ask you: When you coming back?"

Jayden rips open the snack-sized bag and rummages through it until he finds a rye chip. He pops it into his mouth, then looks up at Chris. "Coming back where?"

"To Hoop Group."

Jayden stops mid-chew. "Who said I was coming back to Hoop Group?"

"Tamika said she was gonna talk to you about it."

"Oh, for real?" Jayden says, now biting into a mini breadstick. "Well she hasn't talked to me. It doesn't matter, though. I'm not coming back."

"Why not?"

Jayden casts his eyes toward one of the clocks suspended from the hallway ceiling. "I'm . . . busy. And I really do gotta go now. For real."

Chris wants to say something else, to press Jayden about why he's not playing with the Ballers or Hoop Group, but when he opens his mouth it's too late. Jayden has already broken into an easy jog, and he's passing Principal Kim's office on his way toward the school's front door.

Chris watches Jayden's silhouette disappear before turning and heading straight to the gym. He is not jogging like Jayden was, but he is in just as much of a hurry.

"Look, I'm sorry," Tamika says when Chris confronts her about his conversation with Jayden. "I never said that I'd already talked to Jayden. You made the suggestion, and I thought it was a good idea. We've been waiting for the right moment, but since you've been coming to practice anyway, I figured you didn't really care that much."

"Sooooo, I'm not supposed to care about playing on a team that only has four players?"

"That's not what I said—"

"Look," Chris says, cutting her off. "I talked to Jayden, and he didn't sound like he was ever coming back. Maybe it's time to figure out plan B."

Tamika balances her basketball on her hip with the crook of her left arm. "Actually, I'm still working on plan A."

"I thought plan A was getting Jayden back on the team."

"*Plan A*," Tamika says, "is to make sure that if we *do* get a fifth player—whether it's Jayden or somebody else—we at least look like a halfway-decent team."

"So . . . more practicing," Anthony says, looking down at the floor.

"Yes. More practicing." Tamika clears her throat. "And I also arranged another scrimmage. It's against Austinberg Prep. . . . tomorrow."

Dex looks as if he's near tears. "Tomorrow! We can't play Austinberg tomorrow! That's your old team! You know how good they are!"

"It's not like we have a lot of other choices," Tamika says flatly.

"Tamika! We couldn't even beat a bunch of ten-year-olds!"

"So we're not supposed to try? Is that what you're saying?"

Dex's "no" is so low that Chris, who's standing right next to him, has to strain to hear it.

"If we lose again, we lose again," Tamika says. "If we have to play four-on-five, we have to play four-on-five. But we're not going to get better unless we play real games. We've come a long way, but we gotta keep going."

And with that, Tamika heads down to the baseline and begins doing lunges toward half-court. Dex and Anthony follow, but they move slowly at first, their legs heavy. Eventually, after a few laps around the gym and a few dribbling drills, they get their steps back. But not Chris. He's just going through the motions, doing the bare minimum.

Tamika watches as Chris breaks for water every couple of minutes, how he takes an extra-long time to transition from one drill to the next. What she doesn't know is that Chris has already decided that this will be his last Hoop Group practice. Once he walks off the Carter Middle School court at 5:00, he plans on never coming back.

Of course, Chris has already considered that Tamika will probably have to cancel the scrimmage when he doesn't show, and the coach and team from Austinberg will probably be very unhappy about traveling all the way to Lorain for nothing. But he doesn't care. *Tamika's smart,* he says to himself. *She'll figure something out.*

After Hoop Group practice, on his way to the Y, Chris is more certain than ever that returning to the Ballers full-time is the right decision. He laughs to himself, thinking about how silly he was to question his father's decision to start this program. Because of Cam King's hustling spirit, Chris doesn't have to stick around while Hoop Group continues to implode. He has *options*.

Chris knows he's late for the Ballers practice, but it's not until he arrives at the Y and sees the clock above the welcome desk that he realizes just how late he is. In her effort to prep for Austinberg, Tamika let Hoop Group practice run about thirty minutes over. Now, instead of showing up an hour into practice like he normally does, Chris arrives just fifteen minutes before the Ballers' practice is scheduled to end.

"Sorry I'm late, Dad," Chris says after joining Cam on the sideline, where he is calling plays during a scrimmage.

Cam only glances at his son before fanning him off. "It's all good. I signed up a couple of new kids at full price, so I need to make sure they get enough playing time anyway."

"Okay . . . That's cool. But I did wanna let you know that today was the last day I had to stay after school. The big test is tomorrow, so now I can be on time to practice."

Cam's eyes are glued to the court. "Chris, it's all good. Just come when you can. If you have something else to do, you have something else to do. Really, it's cool."

"So you don't want me to come to practice?"

Finally, Cam turns and looks at Chris. He looks right *through* him, in fact.

"I never said that I don't want you to come to practice, but you haven't been here, so we had to make do. Honestly, we just don't really *need* you right now."

It's amazing how quickly a mind and heart can change, how fast the world can take your hopes and dreams, crush them, and bury them deep. By the time Chris's feet hit the pavement outside the YMCA entrance, his perspective on the Ballers has taken a full turn.

And now he has no options. Tomorrow he will have to show up at Hoop Group practice again, like he never left at all.

CHAPTER 17

"HEY," CHARLENE BAILEY SAYS to Tamika as the rest of the Austinberg Eagles file into the Carter Middle School gym. "It's been a minute."

Tamika looks over at her former teammates, their hair gathered in identical buns at the napes of their necks, all clad in steel-gray warm-up jackets and breakaway pants. "Yeah, it has," she says. "Y'all look good, though."

Tamika follows Charlene's eyes as Charlene takes in the ragtag Hoop Groupers, stretching in their reversible pinnies recycled from three seasons ago. Tamika's expecting pity, which would be perfectly understandable, but all Charlene gives her is a tight smile.

"Where's your dad?" Charlene says after several awkward moments. "He's the coach, right?"

Tamika feels her stomach start to churn. Charlene used to be her best friend, but they haven't talked in months, not since Tamika found out she wasn't going back to Austinberg. Even when she decided to schedule this scrimmage, she had Principal Kim reach out to Coach Leslie at Austinberg instead of hitting up Coach Leslie or Charlene herself. She assumed it would be easy to cut away all traces of her former life, but now Tamika has to endure the clumsiness of a conversation with someone who was once so close.

Though the time lost between them is technically short, the months apart already feel like years. Tamika can't tell Charlene about her father's Parkinson's. She can't tell her that most of the decent players at Carter Middle left Hoop Group as soon as he stepped down. And she definitely can't tell her that, at the moment, her relationship with her father is a full-blown disaster. So Tamika just returns Charlene's smile and says that everything is great, that Hoop Group is a solid crew ready to defend their home court.

"Well, I hope y'all have a good game," Charlene says. "Let us know if you want to take a longer break at halftime since you guys only have four players and nobody to sub."

"Uh, thanks," Tamika says, slightly ashamed, "but I think we'll be okay."

"Okay, then," Charlene says. "See you on the sideline."

As Tamika sets up at center court for the jump ball to start the game, Jayden slips in the gym door and slides into the shadows, careful not to be seen. He watches silently as Tamika tips the ball back to Dex, gasps as Dex fumbles the ball right into the hands of Austinberg's point guard, and grimaces as the Austinberg player converts the turnover into an easy layup.

It doesn't take long for Jayden to realize that Austinberg is a really good team. They're shooting lights-out from the field, making easy buckets on fast breaks, running the court and running up the score. Hoop Group never gives up. Tamika draws up a couple of plays that pull Austinberg's best defenders toward her and Chris, leaving Anthony open for some high-percentage baskets in the paint. On defense, Dex is like a little gnat, swarming Austinberg's point guard, and forcing her to make a few wild passes.

With just a few minutes left in the game, Jayden is impressed that Hoop Group continues to play hard even though the game is obviously out of reach. He watches as Chris cuts to the basket, catching a pass from Tamika and then kicking the ball out to Dex. Dex is standing well outside of his own shooting range, but he eyes a wide-open lane to the goal, puts the ball on the floor, and drives. It should be an easy layup—Dex's first Hoop Group bucket *ever*—but then, out of nowhere, an Austinberg forward flies in from the wing and flattens him.

It's a hard foul that leaves Dex sprawling and his glasses clattering across the floor. Without thinking, Jayden takes a step forward, ready to defend his teammate. Then he remembers that he's not anyone's teammate, not anymore. He checks himself and steps back to where he can't be seen as Dex climbs to his feet and grabs his specs. Tamika sees the bright red gash on Dex's cheek and starts to walk toward him, but before she's even taken two steps, Dex is standing at the free-throw line, ball in hand.

"I think that's two!" Dex says just before bringing the ball low between his legs and then launching it granny-style toward the basket. He drains the first free throw. The second—another *swish*—comes moments later.

Unfortunately, neither Dex's tenacity nor his perfect free throws are enough to keep the Hoop Groupers in the game. The final score is 42–24, Austinberg. It's a tough loss for the Hoop Groupers, but it's one that they can feel good about. It's also enough to show Jayden that maybe Hoop Group still has some life left after all.

When Jayden decided to stop by the gym, he didn't expect to feel the weird mix of longing and desire that's now gnawing at his chest. Tamika, Anthony, Dex, and Chris might have lost their game, but they lost as a team—a much-improved team that has something to fight for. And even though Jayden is still hooping at the Blocks every morning, that's not this. That's not setting picks for teammates, curling around defenders to hit a jumper on the move, banding together to dig out of a hole in a game's final minutes.

This is basketball, and after watching his former teammates, Jayden realizes that he misses it much more than he thought he did.

CHAPTER 18

THE NEXT DAY, Jayden arrives at Slice at 4:20 and spends the slow hours before the dinner rush working on homework and refilling Parmesan cheese and red pepper shakers. By 6:00, he is bussing tables, balancing a gray tub on his hip and tossing in plates of half-eaten garlic knots and overdressed salads.

As he cycles back and forth from the dining room to the kitchen, Jayden decides to turn the task of clearing tables into a personal challenge. Before every trip around the dining room, he checks the clock on the pizza oven and logs the time in his mind, then he checks it as soon as he walks back into the kitchen. The goal: to get faster every time.

The left half of the dining room is typically the quickest to clear. The bar takes up most of the space; the rest is filled with a half-dozen bar-height tables. With their seating for two and tendency to attract customers who only order appetizers, cleanup is relatively easy. It's the right half of the restaurant that presents the biggest challenges and makes it nearly impossible for Jayden to beat his best time. It's where the larger groups are typically seated—the birthday parties and the families with toddlers who throw pepperoni on the floor and sprinkle salt on the table. That side is *much* harder to clean.

Jayden is wiping a puddle of ranch dressing off a chair—the last step before he can drop his tub in the kitchen and start the next round—when Tamika, Anthony, Chris, and Dex sit down at a four-top in the middle of the restaurant.

He didn't see them come in, but the voice he hears call out his name is unmistakable. Jayden looks up to see Anthony standing at their table, his hands cupped around his mouth in a makeshift megaphone.

"Shh! You're being too loud," Tamika says to him, and Anthony slinks back into his seat next to her without another word.

Reluctantly, Jayden drops his rag into the tub and heads over to their table, dirty dishes in tow.

"How long have you been working here?" Dex asks as Jayden steps up next to their table.

Jayden glances over his shoulder to make sure Roddy isn't watching. "I don't know. A couple weeks, I guess?"

"Wow," Dex says. "I thought you weren't at Hoop Group practices because you were playing with the Ballers."

Jayden notices how Chris's face falls at the mention of his dad's new team, but he's got his own issues to deal with. "Nah, man," he says to Dex. "I've been here at the restaurant."

Jayden anticipates that one of them is going to ask why he never said anything about his new job, and his muscles go rigid as a result.

"So," Dex says, "if you're not playing with the Ballers, does that mean you can come back to Hoop Group?"

Jayden breathes a slight sigh of relief. Dex's question doesn't have an easy answer either, but at least it's not the question Jayden thought they would ask.

"I wish I could," Jayden says solemnly.

"Why can't you?"

"Why don't you mind your business?" Tamika says,

elbowing Dex as her eyes flash with embarrassment.

"It's cool," Jayden says to the group, and to Tamika specifically. "My mom lost her job, so I've been working here in the afternoons to help out. I don't make a whole lot, but every little bit counts."

"Dang, Jayden," Dex says. "I . . . I didn't know."

Jayden shrugs. "It's cool."

"You sure?" Anthony asks. He knows too well how quickly "cool" can spiral into "not cool" and then, even quicker, to "terrible."

"Yeah, we are," Jayden mumble-says. "I mean, that's what my mom and Grams said. Grams owns her house, so it's not like if we miss a payment we'll get kicked out, like if we were renting. I think, like, if you're paying a mortgage, you get more time from the bank or something. It's like, three or four months before they foreclose."

"Yeah, I think you're right," Tamika says, nodding, even though she's never once worried about whether she'd have a home and really has no clue how those things actually work.

Jayden smiles to keep the water that is pooling in his eyes from falling. He hates talking about his family like this, like his mom is some kind of helpless victim. Really, she's the strongest person he knows. She sacrificed so much to raise Jayden. Now, instead of making even tiny steps forward, she's on the brink of losing every-thing.

"I'm so sorry that happened to your mom, and I totally get why you can't come back to Hoop Group right now," Tamika says. "But if things ever . . . *change*, just . . . just know we'll always have a spot for you."

Jayden nods and says thank you. Then, with his eyes burning from salty tears, he gathers his tub and gets back to work.

Back in the Slice kitchen, Jayden hands a stack of plates to the dishwasher and turns around to find Roddy stand-ing right behind him.

"Looks like you're all caught up on your tables," he says. "If you got a second, I wanna holla at you real quick."

Jayden is worried that he may be in trouble for talking to his friends while he's on the clock, but he says "sure" and follows Roddy out the back door of the restaurant.

Once outside, they both lean their bodies against the cool brick wall of the building just as the sun begins its final descent beneath the horizon.

"I heard you talking to your friends in there," Roddy says.

"Yeah. I'm sorry. It was only for a minute—"

"Nah, nah, I'm not mad," Roddy says, waving a hand. "I heard what you were talking about, though." He stops and strokes his goatee. "I already told you there ain't nothing wrong with you stepping up to take care of your family, and I meant that. You're doing a good thing—for your mom and your grandma. But if you don't remember anything else I tell you, I want you to remember this: you can't get so caught up in the right now that you lose sight of the future."

Jayden's forehead bunches with confusion. "I don't know what you mean."

Roddy takes a deep breath, rubs his palms together, and tells Jayden about the moment when he and his high school girlfriend found out she was pregnant, how, as her belly began pressing tight against the front of her cheerleading uniform, he was forced to make the most important decision of his life.

"What did you do?" Jayden says.

"What do you think I did?"

"Well, I remember that after you and Kendrick graduated from Willow Brook, we didn't really hear about you playing in college or anything. I always wondered what happened to you, so I'm guessing you quit playing."

"That's exactly what happened," Roddy says. "I had full-ride offers to Duke and UCLA, my dream schools, but I couldn't imagine leaving my daughter or my girl. So I stayed in Lorain. I got a job at Top Burger and used my checks to pay rent and buy diapers."

Jayden nods. "I hear what you're saying, and it sounds like you did the right thing. But I also feel like you wouldn't be telling me this if you didn't feel like you had made the wrong choice."

Roddy shakes his head. "Nah. That ain't it. I'mma say it again: it's never wrong to take care of your family. I'm just saying that what I did wasn't the only way I could have taken care of my family."

"I don't get it."

"It's like this," Roddy says. "I wanted to study architecture so I could learn to build affordable housing that was actually nice, not like the crappy roach-infested projects I grew up in. I was going to play pro ball and invest the money I made into a real estate company. Then I was going to develop housing complexes that would make it so other kids didn't have to grow up the way I did. That was the plan that was gonna help me take care of my family *and* help me become the person God called me to be. But not going to school meant that I wasn't hooping at all, so I couldn't get to the League. And since I was working at Top Burger instead of studying architecture, I couldn't pursue that part of my dream, either."

"Oh," Jayden says softly. "I see what you mean. But, like, if you had gone to school all the way in California, who would've taken care of your family?"

"That's a good question, and it's a question that I didn't have the answer to back then. I really don't have the answer now, either. I just wish I would've had more faith, like my grandpa always said."

"Faith in what?"

"Faith in God, faith in family, faith in the idea that I wouldn't have been born with certain gifts if I wasn't meant to use them. Before he died, my grandpa was always telling me not to worry. He always said everything was gonna work itself out, even if it felt impossible at the time. He wanted me to go to school, and he said that my girl and the baby coulda stayed with him at his house if necessary, but I just wasn't trying to hear it. My dad was never around for me, so I wanted to be there for my kid. I didn't consider that the best way to be there for her was to become the best version of myself."

"So is this about me playing basketball?" Jayden says, his eyes cast somewhere far in the distance.

"Yes and no. It's about you doing what you feel called to do. Might be basketball, might be something else. Might be basketball *and* something else. You're twelve, and I know basketball is all you can see yourself doing right now, and that's cool. Basketball might be the thing that gets you into prep school and college so that you can discover another dream that's just as important and that can also help you get your mom off the couch. Who knows? I just want you to be open to all of it. I want you to consider every single opportunity that's available to you, and I want you to go after them with everything you got in you."

Roddy pauses and cocks his head just slightly. "Yo, you ever been on a plane before?"

"Nah," Jayden says. "My mom said we were gonna fly to Disney World for spring break one year, but then she ended up having to work."

"Man, I'm sorry to hear that," Roddy says. "Disney's dope, but I actually asked you that because, whenever you do take a flight, before the plane takes off, the flight attendants are gonna come out and give you all the safety rules. They're gonna tell you how to put on your seat belt and where the exit rows are, and they're gonna tell you what to do if the cabin pressure starts to decline."

"Okay," Jayden says, even though he has no idea what Roddy is talking about.

"Basically, the flight attendants tell you that if the cabin suddenly loses pressure, it'll be hard to breathe and oxygen masks will drop down from the ceiling."

"And you're supposed to put the mask on, right?"

"Exactly," Roddy says. "And you're supposed to do that *before* you help anybody else put their masks on. Even if you're flying with your young kids or your old grandparents. You put *your* oxygen mask on *first*."

"But what if your kid is like a year old or something? A baby can't put his own mask on."

"That's true, and you can help them. But not until

you've put your own mask on first."

Jayden searches his mind for understanding but comes up short. "How come?"

"Well" Roddy says with a smile, "you can't save anybody else's life if you're already dying."

CHAPTER 19

IT'S BEEN A HALF HOUR since Tamika left Slice, but Jayden is still on her mind. His willingness to give up basketball to work a part-time job for his family was an awakening for all the Hoop Groupers, but Tamika carries it especially close. The bond between Jayden and his mother is like a high-beam flashing a spotlight into the emptiness that looms between her and Coach Beck.

Recent events may have brought new hurts and disappointments, but Tamika and her father haven't been close in years. For as long as she can remember, basketball took him away and kept him away, on long nights in town and longer weekends on the road. There was always some player on his team that he was grooming—Kendrick King, then the next Kendrick King, then the next one after that.

All the while, Tamika developed her own game, working dribbling drills in the driveway and studying shooting mechanics on YouTube. She laughs now, remembering how Dex pegged her form to Coach Beck, how Dex has no idea that Tamika learned it by watching some of her father's old film, and not from the man himself.

Tamika always assumed that she'd grow closer to her father as her game improved, that they'd bond over motion offenses and zone defenses. Only recently did she come to understand that, no matter how hard she tried or how good she got, her games would never mean as much to her dad as Hoop Group's. It wasn't that he didn't like female athletes; he just didn't believe they had a future in basketball.

Women's hoops will never be as popular as men's, he'd told her when she turned ten. *Unless you play college ball at one of a handful of schools, you'll be playing in front of empty seats. There's no future for girls playing basketball.*

But what if I'm good enough to play at UConn? she'd countered. *What if Geno Auriemma comes all the way to Lorain to see me play?*

Coach Beck had simply shrugged. *Okay. So you play for UConn. Let's say you even get drafted into the WNBA after that. Then what? You'll make, what, $75,000 a year? You'll have to spend your whole off-season playing in different countries just to piece together an income that's still a fraction of the NBA league minimum. What's the point? You can go to med school or law school and make two or three times that.*

Tamika had no response. She hadn't realized that the women made so much less than the men in pro basketball, but this information only made her want to play more. It made her want to make the WNBA better for other girls like her, not avoid it completely. Meanwhile, her dad was busy trying to push her into tennis, a sport where women like Serena make more than a lot of the men. It was too late, though. Tamika was already in love with basketball, and the chasm between her and her father seemed to become permanent.

Those memories are fresh, the wounds still raw, but as Tamika arrives back home and walks past the kitchen on the way to her bedroom, she comes face-to-face with the reality that the past problems she's had with her father may not matter anymore.

"He won't eat," Tamika's mother says through tears.

"How's he going to fight this thing if he won't even eat?"

Tamika studies the plate on the table where her dad normally sits. Baked chicken, smashed sweet potatoes, and roasted broccoli remain untouched.

"He just stares at me," her mother continues. "When I talk to him, he just stares like I'm not even saying anything."

Tamika takes a couple of deep breaths and tries to summon enough calm for herself and her mom. "Did you call the doctor?"

"I did. He said that this is normal, but nothing about it feels normal to me. He said Parkinson's patients sometimes have a hard time swallowing and that I should make your dad some softer foods. So I did that. I made your dad sweet potatoes and he wouldn't even try them. I don't know what to do. He can't *not eat*." Sobs devour the rest of her words and she buries her face in her hands.

When her mother first told her about her father's diagnosis, Muhammad Ali was Tamika's sole reference point. He was the only person Tamika knew who'd ever had the disease, and although she's never told her mother, that realization has been the source of many nightmares. When Tamika thinks of Ali, she thinks of him at the end of his life—wheelchair-bound and silent, the confident swagger of his youth stolen by this horrible sickness.

With her own voice thick with emotion, Tamika asks her mother, "Will Daddy end up like Muhammad Ali?"

Tamika's mother rises from the table, walks over to Tamika, and wraps her baby in her arms.

"Maybe you should try to talk him," she tells Tamika, and then adds with a smile, "He always listens to you, even if it doesn't always seem like it."

Tamika finds Coach Beck in the den with ESPN muted on the big screen and a scrapbook of old newspaper clippings open on his lap. She walks up behind him, and when she does, she notices his finger lingering over the same article that Dex had mentioned. There she is atop her father's broad shoulders, her messy pigtails bound with giant baubles, her grin too big for her baby face. She can't recall the moment when the picture was taken, or even that day, but she remembers how she felt—how she *knew*—that her father was the greatest guy in the whole world. She smiles at the thought.

Moments later, Coach Beck senses Tamika standing

behind him. He's startled when he turns around and sees her, but he also seems happy to have her there.

"Come have a seat," he says as he points to a nearby chair. "Why don't you tell me how Hoop Group's been going?"

"Everything's good," she says, pleased that her father is willing to talk about basketball. "I think we may be finding our rhythm."

Coach Beck nods. "What about Jayden?"

Tamika's heart seizes at the memory of his words at Slice. "Um, he left Hoop Group, actually, and he's not playing basketball at all right now. He's, um . . . dealing with some stuff at home."

"Hmm," Coach Beck says. "That's too bad."

"It is, but we'll be fine. Dex and Anthony are still learning, but I'm there. And we have Chris, too."

"Chris?!" Coach Beck slaps the arm of his recliner and shakes his head. "Chris isn't a team player. He thinks he's a leader but he doesn't know the first thing about leadership."

"You're right, Dad," Tamika says. "But it's fine, 'cause I'm the captain right now. I'm leading the team."

Coach Beck stares silently at his daughter.

"I got Principal Kim to come on as the adult supervisor," Tamika continues. "She's even arranged scrimmages against other teams."

Tamika stops, suddenly thinking about Dex's suggestion that she ask Coach Beck to pop into practice once a week to help drive sign-ups. They definitely need another body if they're going to have any shot at competing in the Fall Invitational, and her recruitment strategy is failing miserably. Maybe Dex was right. Maybe her father would be willing to help Hoop Group secure a fifth player.

Tamika starts telling Coach Beck about Hoop Group's current predicament and how she's done everything she can to fix it. He appears to be listening, but all of a sudden, before she can even ask for help, Coach Beck is standing, gripping his chair with one hand for balance and pointing the other at Tamika's face.

"Who do you think you are?" he says to her as droplets of spittle fly from his mouth. "You all have no right. No right!"

"No right for what, Daddy?"

"No right to enter the tournament as Hoop Group!"

"Well, I'm sorry," Tamika says sarcastically, "but we

are Hoop Group now."

Coach Beck cuts his eyes at her. "Watch your tone, young lady. I've worked my whole life to make a name for that program. I will *not* have it ruined just because you want to play around—"

"Play around? Nobody's playing around!"

"I told y'all on the first day that I had to step down and there wouldn't be a program this year. But you just had to go behind my back anyway. And for what? You don't even have enough kids for a real team!"

Coach Beck coughs, clears his throat, and settles back in his chair before adding, "Shut it down, Tamika. Shut it down now."

Tamika is near tears, but she holds them back long enough to tell her father, more respectfully this time, that it's too late. The Shoot, Dunk, and Spin Classic is a series of skills challenges held at the end of the Lakeside Fall Festival, and the winning team gets an automatic entry into the Fall Invitational. Tamika has already entered the team, and she signed them up as Hoop Group from Carter Middle School.

"Whatever," Coach Beck says, turning back to his scrapbook. "You can call your little team whatever you want, but you'll never win the Classic, and you'll never be the real Hoop Group."

Later that night, Tamika is crying herself to sleep when her mom comes in to tell her good night.

"I just don't understand," Tamika sobs. "He's just so mean to me."

"I'm so sorry, baby," her mom says. "Your dad's just not himself right now. He's sick."

"Well, what am I supposed to do? Accept the fact that he doesn't care about me or my dreams just because he's sick?"

Tamika's mother sits on the edge of her bed and pulls Tamika close to her, rubbing her daughter's back in tiny, soothing circles. "No, baby," she says. "You're supposed to go out there and keep fighting. You're supposed to show your father—and everyone else—that you can go out there and *win*."

CHAPTER 20

BASKETBALL IS MORE THAN *a game to me. It is my life.*

Jayden looks down at the page, reads the line two more times.

No. That's not it.

He erases it, tries again.

When everything goes wrong, I know that playing basketball will always be right.

Nope.

Still not right.

Jayden scratches his head and twirls his pencil between two fingers. Then he tries again.

No matter what has gone on in my life, basketball has never given up on me. So I can't ever give up on basketball.

Jayden studies the newest words printed on top of the eraser marks from his previous attempts. He doesn't love them, but he doesn't hate them, either.

It is the morning of the Shoot, Dunk, and Spin Classic, and Jayden is trying to keep his mind off the fact that he's not participating by finishing his Creative Writing assignment. It's not really working.

Though it's not as significant as the Fall Invitational, the Classic is still a big deal in Lorain. It's a who's who of the best young players in the region, an opportunity for kids to try out new tricks and polish old ones, hopefully landing on the radar of an AAU or prep coach in need of a few budding stars. And that's to say nothing of the prizes. They can win sneakers, jerseys, tickets to Ohio State basketball games, and, of course, the championship team gets an automatic entry into the Fall Invitational Tournament.

Jayden had been looking forward to dominating the competition this year, to turning the Classic into his personal hoops coming out party before he heads off to Willow Brook. Instead, he's at home, sweating through the first draft of his essay.

Jayden is giving it a final read when Grams makes her

way to the coffeemaker.

"What you workin' on over there, Jayden?" she says. "It's not like you to be doing homework early on a Saturday."

"Yeah," Jayden says, still staring at the words on the paper in front of him. "I'mma go down to the Blocks later, but I wanted to finish this essay for school first."

Grams has just scooped the grounds into the top of the machine, but she doesn't even close the lid before sliding over to the kitchen doorway and holding out her hand. "Let me see it."

"Um. It's not really ready yet. I can let you read it when—"

"Naw," Grams says, cutting him off. "You gon' let me read it now. Or did you forget that I was an English teacher for thirty-two years?"

Jayden sighs and hands over three sheets of loose-leaf notebook paper. Grams then sets them on the kitchen table while she finishes making her coffee. Once her mug is full, she sits and reads. Very, very slowly.

Impatient, Jayden walks into the kitchen and stands right behind Grams.

"Boy, I know you don't think I'm 'bout to let you stand over my shoulder while I'm reading."

"I was just trying to see how much you have left."

Grams takes her glasses off and sets them on the table before turning in her seat to look at Jayden directly. "Actually," she says, "I just finished."

Jayden feels his stomach knotting and tries to keep it loose with slow, deep breaths. "And? What did you think?" Then: "It must be bad. I knew it was bad. I've been working on it all morning, but it's just not coming together the way I—"

"No, baby," Grams says as she lays a gentle hand on his forearm. "It's not bad at all. It's fantastic, actually, and I'm so proud of you for writing it."

Grams motions to the chair next to her, telling Jayden to sit. "Look, Jayden," she says. "There are a whole lot of people who would tell you that making it to the NBA is a real long shot and you should probably choose a career with better odds. But I'm not gon' tell you that."

"You're not?"

"No, I'm not. I happen to think that big dreams are the best dreams."

Jayden smiles as his chest fills with warmth.

"You're right for holding tight to that dream, Jayden. It's yours, and you aren't obligated to change it for anybody." Grams smiles back, then adds, "When this life is all over, you're gonna have to answer for you and only you. So you better make sure you got something good to say."

Jayden laughs, says, "Grams, you sound just like Roddy."

"And who is Roddy?"

"Roddy is the guy who owns Slice, the pizza place where I work. He played at Willow Brook back in the day. He was on the same team as Kendrick King."

"*Hmph.* Well, I still don't *know* this Roddy person, but if he sounds like me, he must know what he's talking about."

Jayden laughs and stands to hug his grandmother. "Thank you, Grams," he says. "For everything."

Grams wraps her arms around Jayden, and as they embrace, she whispers in his ear: "God never promised that this life would be easy, Jayden. Everybody has something they gotta overcome, even that Kendrick King you love so much. But what sets the successful apart from the not so successful is their stubbornness. They already know they gon' win the game before it even starts, and you can't tell 'em otherwise. That's the kinda spirit you gotta have."

Just then, the cordless phone sitting next to the microwave rings, and Jayden breaks away from Grams to answer it. To his surprise, it's Roddy.

Roddy apologizes for calling on a Saturday and explains that he has an emergency that can't wait. "Slice is gonna have a booth at the Lakeside Fall Festival," he says. "I was gonna have Deonte work with Lyric and Miko, but he called in sick. You think you can fill in for him?"

Jayden hesitates—since Grams has given his essay her English-teacher seal of approval, he was just about to go hoop—but Roddy offers to pay twice his hourly rate. Jayden quickly agrees, even though he knows he'll be working in the same spot where the Shoot, Dunk, and Spin Classic will be held. He doesn't want to have to watch other kids balling while he's stuck serving slices of pepperoni and cheese. But he also can't afford to pass up double time.

"Absolutely," Jayden says. "I can be there in thirty minutes."

On his way out the door, he grabs his backpack and throws in a pair of basketball shorts and his Kendrick Kings. He may not be able to participate in the Classic, but as soon as he's done working, he's heading straight to the Blocks.

CHAPTER 21

WHEN THE HOOP GROUPERS arrive for the Shoot, Dunk, and Spin Classic, the crowds on the shores of Lake Erie are massive. Adults and children alike are snacking on funnel cakes, clutching stuffed animals won at the game booths, and generally enjoying an unseasonably warm day at the Lakeside Fall Festival.

As Hoop Group's captain, Tamika checks in for the team and is given a sheet of paper that explains the rules for the day's events:

Hoop Group will compete in five different challenges for their age bracket: the three-point contest, the layup showdown, the fast pass, the free-throw contest, and the vertical leap-off. Each team puts one player in each of the five contests, and no player can compete in more than one contest.

Tamika reads and rereads the last line: *Each team puts one player in each of the five contests, and no player can compete in more than one contest.*

This is obviously a huge challenge for the still four-person Hoop Group, but Tamika has already prepared. Even though they don't have enough members to compete in each contest, she has calculated that, if Hoop Group takes first place in the first four contests, they might be able to forfeit the fifth competition and still have enough cumulative points to win. It's a high-risk strategy, to be sure, but it's the only one they have.

First up is the three-point contest. When she, Anthony, Chris, and Dex were deciding who would compete in which event, appointing Tamika to the battle of the long-range shooters was a no-brainer. Tamika knows she's money anywhere behind the arc: in either corner, on the wings, straightaway. No matter where she stands she's nothing but net.

Four volunteers roll out racks of basketballs for Tamika and the three other kids in her heat. On their turns, they each get five attempts at each of five spots on the court.

As the first contestant begins, Tamika quickly realizes that he does his best work from the top of the arc. He hits four of five there, but he only picks up three more baskets during the entire rest of his turn, giving him a total of seven points. The second kid is a little better, and he moves into the lead when he makes nine threes out of twenty-five attempts. Finally, it's Tamika's turn.

Tamika sinks only one basket from the rack in the left corner, and as she moves to the left wing, she wishes she had taken more time to warm up. The second rack is a little better—she hits two of five—but she really heats up at the straightaway position. There, Tamika makes four shots, giving her a total of six as she heads toward the last two racks. She needs only three to tie the current leader, but Tamika isn't interested in tying. She wants to move into the lead—and she wants to lead big.

On the right wing, Tamika's emotions get the best of her. She scores on the first two shots, but she's anxious going into the last three. Just one more bucket would move her into a tie for first, but she puts too much on her shot and all three ricochet off the backboard.

Now she's at the last rack—the right corner, her favorite spot on the court. She takes two deep breaths, picks up the ball, and takes a couple of dribbles.

She lets the ball fly, and the crowd cheers as the first ball pops through the net.

Her second shot is money, too, sliding effortlessly through the rim.

Shots three and four are more of the same, and now Tamika's only objective is sinking the last shot and finishing her turn with a perfect five for five.

Tamika takes two more dribbles and lets her knees bounce as she sinks into her heels. She eyes the back of the rim and then aims for an imaginary spot just inside it, just like her father always taught his players. Then she shoots.

Swish!

Tamika makes seven of her last ten shots for a total of thirteen during the round. It's good enough to move her into first place—all by herself.

The Hoop Groupers have secured their first contest victory, but there is no time to celebrate. They must move quickly to the next three, starting with the layup showdown, which pits each competitor against an obstacle course of cones, ropes, and defender dummies.

To win, the player must stay on their feet and avoid the challenges while driving to the basket. Points are only counted if the layup is made, and the more creative the drive—the more twists and turns the shooter can incorporate—the more points they get.

Chris is the Hoop Group representative in the layup showdown, and his first of three allowed attempts is perfect. He doesn't touch any of the cones or the dummy defender, and on his drive, he comes in at the perfect angle to sink a right-handed shot. The judges give him a score of seven out of ten.

On his second drive, Chris is even better. This time, he scores an eight.

The problem is Chris's last attempt. A couple of extra cones are set up to increase the difficulty, and Chris nearly dribbles right into one. As a result, his balance is off as he heads to the goal, and when he puts up the shot, it rattles around and rolls right off the rim. Chris gets zero points for his last layup and finishes the competition in third place.

Though Chris is devastated, Tamika assures him that everything may still be fine. But that's if—and *only if*—they can score perfectly in the next two battles. There's no more room for error.

Anthony readies himself for the fast-pass contest. He'll have sixty seconds to hit as many targets as possible, some that are close and others that are far away, thus requiring incredible arm strength and aim. The reward for hitting the bull's-eye on targets that are farther away is obviously more points, and Anthony begins aiming for them. In theory, this is a smart plan, because no one throws harder than him. But time after time, Anthony picks the ball up and hurls it with all his strength—and not a bit of accuracy.

Like Chris, Anthony slides down the leaderboard and ends up in the middle of the pack.

At this point, Hoop Group's only hope rests on Dex's narrow frame. He'll be competing in the free-throw competition, primarily because the only two options remaining are that contest and the vertical leap-off, and Dex can't exactly *jump*.

On the court's sideline, Anthony, Chris, and Tamika are huddled together, reciting every prayer they've ever learned. If Dex doesn't win, there's no way the team can take home the gold. If the Hoop Groupers don't win the Shoot, Dunk, and Spin Classic, they won't get an automatic bid for the Fall Invitational. And with their team of four, Tamika knows they'd never be able to advance through the qualifying tournament.

Thankfully, Dex doesn't disappoint. Still shooting grandma style, he drains seventeen shots in a row. The second-place finisher locks in eleven baskets, not even close to the kid with the Rick Barry technique.

When Dex comes off the court, he's so excited about his performance and Hoop Group's second first-place victory that he's nearly floating. Tamika, however, is suddenly sullen. She's recalculated the scores and discovered that, not only do the Hoop Groupers have to compete in the vertical leap-off contest, but if they want to take first overall, they may need another first-place victory.

This is impossible, of course. Hoop Group still has only four players, and the rule that none of the athletes can compete in more than one event is rock solid.

As the reality of their failure sets in, Anthony, Dex, and Chris begin untying their sneakers, ready to slip on their slides and head home for the day. Tamika is frozen in place, though, her anger and frustration burning hot in her chest. She hates that her dad was right, that maybe her Hoop Group is just a second-rate version of the program he created. And she hates that now, for the first time in decades, Hoop Group won't be able to compete in the Fall Invitational Tournament.

Tamika's vision is starting to blur as water clouds her eyes, but when she begins walking toward the judges' table to let them know that her team will have to forfeit, she can just barely make out an image of a kid running toward the table at full speed. She blinks back her tears.

Once again, Tamika can see clearly, and she can see exactly who is running toward her.

It's Jayden!

CHAPTER 22

JAYDEN MAY HAVE BEEN HOPING to avoid the Shoot, Dunk, and Spin Classic, but there was no way he could. The Slice booth was positioned right off the main court, the spot where most of the action was taking place. It was prime real estate for selling lots of pizza but a horrible location for someone feeling as court-sick as Jayden.

Naturally, Jayden couldn't *not* watch the competition. He was drawn to it like Kareem Abdul-Jabbar to the playoffs, and in between refilling drinks and clearing trash from the nearby picnic tables, he was silently praying that Hoop Group could squeak out a win.

He saw Chris's missed layups and Anthony's errant

passes, and he knew that even Tamika's and Dex's wins in their respective events weren't going to be enough to push Hoop Group to the top of the standings. They needed a fifth player, someone who could compete in—and *win*—the vertical leap-off.

"Seems like your team could use you," Roddy said to Jayden as soon as the free-throw competition was over.

Jayden shrugged.

"I'm just saying, Lyric, Miko, and me could probably hold it down in here while you go whoop up on some kids in the vertical leap-off." Roddy paused, let a sly smile creep across his lips. "I mean, that's if you're ready, though."

"I *stay* ready," Jayden said, pointing to his backpack on the floor of their booth.

Roddy's smile grew bigger. "Well, I guess you better hurry up and get out there."

Jayden ran off behind the row of food vendors, tore off his hat and apron, and changed from his khakis to his basketball shorts. Then, while still stuffing his feet into his Kendrick Kings, he ran-hopped to the judges' table and managed to get there just before Tamika arrived to admit Hoop Group defeat.

"I'm the fifth member of Hoop Group!" Jayden says, winded and panting. "I'll be competing in the vertical leap-off."

He can feel Tamika's eyes boring though him, but he ignores her. At the moment, his only focus is getting back on the court.

One of the judges, an older man with a balding head and a fuchsia bow tie, begins looking over the registration lists that contain all the names of the kids competing that day. Minutes pass as he scans each roster once, then twice. "I'm sorry, son," the man says, finally, "but what did you say your name was?"

"Jayden Carr."

Jayden holds his breath while the man turns back to his lists.

"I'm really sorry," the man says again, "but I just don't see your name here. And if you're not on the registration sheet, you can't compete. Those are the rules."

Jayden is already turning to walk away from the table when another voice cuts through the suspense like lightning through the darkness of a stormy night. He spins around and discovers that the voice is coming from a different judge, a younger woman with a pixie haircut.

"Technically, Mr. Copeland, the only registration list we're required to consider is the team list from the beginning of their season," she says.

"Huh," Mr. Copeland says. "Are you sure about that, Ms. Taylor? I don't remember that being a rule."

Ms. Taylor rolls her eyes and hands him a spiral-bound red notebook that reads Shoot, Dunk, and Spin Classic on the cover. Mr. Copeland consults the table of contents at the front of the book, flips to the applicable page, and reads. Minutes later, he is apparently satisfied. "Well, it appears that you're right . . . this time." He then pulls out another folder that Jayden assumes must hold each of the team's early-season rosters.

As Mr. Copeland fumbles with the papers, Jayden thinks back to that first day of Hoop Group in the Carter Middle School gym, the day that Coach Beck stepped down and everything changed. If someone had given him the year's forecast over the summer, back when he was still sweating on the Blocks and bodying dudes twice his size, Jayden would have never believed that his seventh-grade year would be like this. He's gone from not playing with Coach Beck to not playing basketball at all, to now standing with his fingers crossed behind his back and hoping that his name made it onto the Hoop Group roster weeks ago.

Mr. Copeland clears his throat. "Mr. Carr, you will be delighted to know that, according to official ruling and Hoop Group's roster from late August, there's nothing stopping you from competing in the vertical leap-off as a representative of this team."

Jayden's head and heart are swimming with excitement, and he immediately starts stretching, lifting each leg behind him, grabbing hold of his ankles, and pulling them tightly toward his butt.

"There is one other thing, though," Mr. Copeland says, interrupting the warm-up. "We can't give you the final okay until your team captain agrees to officially list you as Hoop Group's entry for the competition."

Jayden hasn't had a single conversation with Tamika since walking out of the gym after his fight with Chris weeks ago. He is aware of this and ready to beg for his life, but Tamika starts talking before he can.

"If you want to come back to Hoop Group, I only have one rule," she tells Jayden. "You can't join now and leave again later. We're here to secure our spot in the Fall Invitational Tournament. That's the only thing that matters, and if you can't commit to that, there's no point in you joining us." She waits a beat. "But if you're in for the whole ride, we can roll."

Jayden thinks about his mom, Grams, and the conversations he's had with Roddy. He's not sure what he's going to do about work, but he recognizes that this is his moment—and he knows he's not going to waste it. "I'm in!" he says.

Tamika turns to the judges, her newfound hope extinguishing all her previous disappointment. Now her face is colored with pure, unbridled joy. "You heard him," she tells the judges. "He's in!"

Minutes later, Jayden is standing on the sideline of the outdoor court, taking deep, calming breaths as a judge goes over the contest rules: *There are six teams competing in the vertical leap-off. The field will be split into two heats of three. Each jumper will get two leaps per round, but only the best score will be counted. The top jumper in each heat will advance to the final round.*

When Jayden's name is called as the first contestant in the first heat, he can taste the pepperoni pizza he ate for lunch start to creep up his esophagus. Competition isn't like standing in line at a buffet: going last is actually an advantage because you have a chance to see how well everyone else does. Without that edge, Jayden knows he's going to have to put up a number that's strong enough to stand on its own.

For his first jump, Jayden is measured at 16.5 inches. It's decent but not great, a reflection of the nervous energy that has made its way from his digestive system to his legs. For jump two, he crouches low, pulls in a giant gulp of air, and then explodes upward as he releases it from his mouth. When he lands back on his feet, he immediately turns to the judge for his score. A 17.5.

Next up in Jayden's heat is Terry Sinclair. Terry used to go to Carter Middle and play for Hoop Group; he was good, too, the perfect swingman who could play the two or the three. Jayden had been looking forward to playing with Terry this year, but his parents moved him out to the suburbs over the summer. Now Terry's playing for Ravensville Middle—a great school with three different science labs, a massage table in the locker room . . . and a "just okay" hoops team.

Terry lines up for his jump, and Jayden's stomach is

rumbling with nerves. He suspects that Terry will put up a good number, and he's still not sure that his own score is high enough to stand. But as it turns out, Jayden has no reason to be nervous. Terry's final score is a 16.

As Terry sulks off the court, all attention turns toward the third and last jumper of Jayden's heat. It's Charlene Bailey from Austinberg Prep.

Now Jayden's really nervous. After watching Hoop Group scrimmage against Austinberg, he knows that Charlene is as good as it gets for seventh-grade ballers, that she's long and strong and can get lifted with ease. She's stretching and taking practice jumps, and all Jayden can think to do is turn his back. If Charlene is going to be the one to knock him out of the competition, he doesn't want to see it go down.

Charlene's first jump is met with some groans and a few *ooh*s, so he assumes that his score has held—at least for now. Moments later, when the crowd falls completely silent, Jayden knows that Charlene is readying for her final jump. The seconds pass, and Jayden can feel the tick-tick-tick of time pounding away in his gut. Finally, just as he begins to wonder how much more he can take, a loud gasp lifts up from the crowd.

Instinctively, Jayden spins around and sees Charlene with her head bowed and her body limp. Her score is 17.25. Just a quarter of an inch below Jayden's.

Jayden wants to celebrate winning his heat, but he knows that it means nothing if he can't pull out a victory in the final round. And securing this W won't be easy. Jayden will be competing against Marcus Cheney, the 6'1" center of the Rebels from nearby Avon Lake. Marcus has at least four inches on Jayden, and while the competition is about vertical leap—not natural height—he can't help but be a little worried.

Thirty minutes later, Jayden is shaking out his legs and pounding his thighs with tight fists as he readies for the decisive round.

Marcus is up first. He is strong; his jumps are powerful; and he lands a final score of . . . 18.

Now it's Jayden's turn, and the same thought he's had since he won his heat is continuing to circle his mind: *What if he already gave all he had to give?*

Jayden wipes his palms on his basketball shorts and prepares for his first jump. *This is it*, he thinks, *this is our only chance to make it to the Fall Invitational.*

He squats low and leaps up high, the entire weight of

Hoop Group's future bearing down on his shoulders.

His score: 17 inches.

Jayden blinks, bewildered. For the first time in the competition, his score has gone *down*. It's exactly what he was afraid of, the numerical proof that he's all tapped out. He's seen enough March Madness tournaments to know that just getting to the Elite Eight or the Final Four isn't enough. Teams also have to make sure they have the juice to win those final rounds, and Jayden isn't sure he has enough left in his tank to overcome Marcus's monster score.

Jayden is running low on confidence, but just off of center court, where he now stands, Dex and Anthony are a two-man cheering section, reminding Jayden that he is more than capable of winning, that he's got the goods to soar right into the winner's circle.

Now the competition is about to begin. It's time for Jayden to push their voices far from his mind so he can focus on his jump. He presses his internal mute button, and the whole world goes silent.

Jayden breathes deep and makes his body go low, low, as low as it will go. And then high. High, high, high. Higher still. A fraction of a second later, Jayden's back on the ground again, his ears overflowing with screams and claps from the crowd.

When Jayden turns to look at the judge, her smile is so wide he doesn't even need to hear the words that are coming out of her mouth, the congratulations that accompany her announcement of his score. Jayden has jumped 18.5 inches, securing a Hoop Group win in the vertical leap-off and first place in the entire Shoot, Dunk, and Spin Classic.

CHAPTER 23

Now THAT JAYDEN IS BACK on the team, it feels like Hoop Group is finally on sure footing, like nothing but good things are ahead for the rest of the season. Anthony and Dex are still developing, of course, but the holes in their games are more than covered by Jayden and Tamika. At the same time, Chris is beginning to settle into his role as the team's perfect utility player. He's learning that he's part of the team but not the *whole* team, that he doesn't need to compete against the kids on his own bench.

It's a good thing, too, because early rounds of the Fall Invitational Tournament kick off just a week after the Classic ends. Thankfully, with its roster in place and its chemistry undeniable, Hoop Group is able to blow through its first few matchups with ease.

Still, there is always a stirring of doubt for Jayden. Since rejoining Hoop Group, he's only able to work on Saturdays and Sundays. His mom and Grams have told him not to worry, but he can't help it now that his weekly pay has been cut in half.

This weighs heavy on Jayden as Hoop Group barrels through the first three rounds of competition, beating the Ravensville Wildcats 39–16, the Tri-City Bulldogs 46–30, and the Akron Avalanche 54–37. And even though he can't stop stressing about how his mom is going to get caught up on her car payments as Hoop Group faces off against the Amherst Trojans, Jayden somehow manages to hit eleven of sixteen from the floor and six of seven from the free-throw line. It's good enough for a total of 28 points, good enough to push his team to a 56–43 win.

In short, basketball is going really, really well—even if Jayden is having a hard time enjoying it.

Jayden has just made it home from Hoop Group practice on an otherwise normal Wednesday when he finds

Grams standing over a giant pot of greens. "What's going on?" he asks.

Grams turns and smiles. "What you mean, 'What's going on?' Maybe I just wanted to cook a good dinner for my family."

Jayden's not buying it. In all his life, Grams has never, ever made greens on a weekday. She always said that greens were weekend work, that it took too much time to clean and chop and cook them low and slow. But now, in the middle of the week, she's got a pot big enough to feed the whole block. On top of that, he can smell her world-famous 7UP cake doing its thing in the oven.

Jayden shakes his head. "Nah, Grams. Something's going on, and you just don't wanna tell me."

This time Grams laughs. "Okay, Jayden," she says. "You might be right. Sit down and let me get you something to drink while I talk to you."

Jayden watches as Grams takes her sweet time pouring him a glass of sweet tea. By the time she places it in front of him, he's too anxious to drink, but he also knows better than to press her. She'll tell him what she has to tell him when she gets good and ready.

Grams checks on the greens again and adds a bit more

water to the pot, along with a couple of dashes of vinegar. Then, before finally sitting down, she removes the cake from the oven and replaces it with a pan of chicken thighs covered in gravy.

"Well," Grams says as she settles into her seat with her own glass of tea, "I wanted to tell you about what happened to me today."

"Okay . . ."

"You don't seem excited to hear my news," Grams says, smirking.

Jayden laughs. "I am. I'm just trying to figure out what you're gonna say."

"Fine," Grams says, laughing again. "I guess I better tell you since you obviously aren't very good at reading minds." She pauses to take a long sip of her tea. "So. I was so inspired by you rejoining Hoop Group and still helping out around here that I decided to go down to Lorain County Library."

"The library?" This is not the news Jayden was expecting.

"Yes, Jayden, the library. Just listen."

"Fine."

"So. I went to the library and asked them if they needed

any help with anything. I've been looking for work, but Lord knows I can't stand on my feet for hours serving pancakes at IHOP or ringing up toilet paper at Target. So I figured the library might need someone to restock shelves or read to kids, especially if that someone loves books and used to teach."

Now Jayden's intrigued. "Well, what'd they say?"

"The little woman sitting at the front desk didn't say much, honestly. She didn't have a clue about jobs, so I asked if I could speak to her manager."

"And?"

"*Aaaaaaand,*" Grams says sarcastically, "the manager said that the library had just gotten funding from the state to launch a county-wide literacy program to teach adults and kids how to read. And they need somebody to run it!"

Grams goes on to say that the manager—*Mr. Tafoya is his name*—told her that she needed to fill out an application online before she could be considered for the role. She walked right over to one of the library's computers and finished the application. Then she went back to talk to Mr. Tafoya.

"He told me he would call to set up an interview, but

let me tell you I wasn't *about* to walk out that library till that man talked to me," Grams says. "He acted like he wanted to say no, but there wasn't a soul in that library besides the three of us, so he couldn't have been that busy. Anyway, we ended up talking for about twenty minutes!"

"Aaaaaaaand," Jayden says.

"And that's it! They're interviewing a couple more candidates and are planning to make their final decision sometime in the next few weeks."

The smile that had been stretching Jayden's lips wide now collapses.

"What's the matter?" Grams asks.

"You don't have the job yet. You won't even know if you got it for weeks. And they're still interviewing other people."

"That's right. What's your point?"

Jayden shakes his head. "I just don't get why you're so happy. Nothing's changed."

"That's not true," Grams says, reaching a hand across the table and placing it on top of Jayden's. "Plenty has changed. Now there is something to hope for, something to put your faith in."

Jayden mumbles under his breath, so low that Grams can't hear him.

"What did you just say?" she says.

"Nothing."

"Naw, you said something, and you better tell me what it is."

Jayden sighs, his eyes welling with tears. "'Nothing' is what I said, Grams. I said that just having something to hope for is nothing. It means nothing."

"Oh, baby," Grams says, her voice soft. "Having hope is everything. The solutions to our problems rarely come as fast as we want them to, and in the meantime, while we wait, it's our hope and our faith that keep us going. It's literally all we got."

"But what if you don't get whatever it is you're hoping for?" Jayden says as fat tears slip down his cheeks. "What do you do then?"

"Well," Grams says. "You just keep hoping."

At Hoop Group practice the next day, Anthony can't help but notice how everyone seems to be in such good spirits because the future of the program seems limitless once again. Anthony shakes his head. He knows that if he hadn't just left Principal Kim's office, he would probably feel that way, too.

Anthony was early for their meeting, a prescheduled check-in before Hoop Group practice began. He waited outside her office like he always did, flipping through the graphic novel version of Kwame Alexander's *The Crossover*. He didn't mean to overhear her talking about the next year's budget, the cost cutting across the district, how there's just no more money for Hoop Group to continue.

But he heard it all, and now he can't unhear it. It's with him, wrapped tight around his insides, weighing him down like an anchor. A few months ago, he wouldn't have given a second thought to Hoop Group being cut; today, he can't imagine a school year without it.

"Hey, Anthony, you good?" Tamika is waving a hand in his face, trying to bring his attention back to the basketball court.

"Hey. Yeah, I'm good."

"You . . . *sure*? You don't seem like it."

Anthony hesitates. He wasn't going to say anything until after practice, maybe when everyone else had left, and he and Tamika were alone. But now he's second-guessing, thinking that perhaps this is as good a time as any.

"I overheard Principal Kim talking to someone in her office," Anthony says. "She was talking about the budget for next year for field trips and extracurricular activities, like sports." He pauses and meets each pair of eyes that are staring back at him. "Basically, this is going to be the last year of Hoop Group."

"Wait, what?" Tamika says. "I don't understand. We finally have a full team and are playing better than ever, and now you're saying that this is it?"

Anthony nods solemnly. "Yeah. I guess so."

"But we still get to finish this season, right?" Chris asks.

Tamika turns and glares at him. "Is that all you're thinking about? What about next year? What about the fact that this program has been around for decades? What about all the work my dad—"

Tamika's words catch in her throat, and at the same time, Principal Kim appears from just behind her. No one had even noticed when she walked into the gym.

"I know you're upset, and you have every right to be, but I want you to know that I did everything I could to save the program," Principal Kim says. "We just don't have the money for Hoop Group to continue. I can't commit to supervising next year, and none of the other teachers are willing to, either. That means we'd have to hire an outside coach, and in addition to the costs for uniforms, travel, tournament fees, and everything else, it's more than Carter Middle can take on."

Tamika nods with understanding, but inside, she's on fire, like someone dropped a lit match down her throat. She's still not ready to give up on Hoop Group. None of the kids are. Not yet at least.

When Principal Kim leaves to take a call in her office, they all gather on the bleachers and begin tossing out potential ideas for saving the program. Nothing seems realistic, though . . . until Dex suggests that Chris reach out to his uncle Kendrick. "He grew up in Hoop Group," Dex says. "Surely he can write a check before letting it fall apart because of a budget shortage."

Like his suggestion that Tamika ask Coach Beck to help drive Hoop Group registrations, Dex's Kendrick King strategy seems perfect on paper, a wild request made reasonable by the existence of family ties. But these things are never, ever, as perfect or as easy as they seem, and even if Dex doesn't understand that, Tamika does. Chris does, too.

For a second, Chris is fully prepared to tell another lie, to make a promise on behalf of his uncle that he knows he can't keep. But this time, he stops himself. He's been spinning stories and telling half-truths his whole life, trying to live up to a version of himself that's based solely on his last name. He doesn't want to do it anymore, and for the first time in his life, Chris feels like he doesn't have to.

"I wish I *could* call my uncle," Chris says, "but I actually haven't spoken to him in a while, not since my dad got him wrapped up in that whole mess with the fake jerseys a few years ago."

The Hoop Groupers are stunned into silence, rendered speechless not just because of the drama between Chris and Kendrick, but also Chris's willingness to admit it.

"Wow," Dex says. "That's . . . a lot."

"Yeah, it really sucks when things are messed up in your own family," Tamika says.

Chris chuckles awkwardly in an attempt to lighten the mood. "It's fine," he says. "Plus, I really ain't trying to talk about all that right now. I thought we came to hoop!"

Tamika exchanges a knowing glance with Chris

and, after only a moment of hesitation, follows his lead in changing the conversation. "Okay, then," she says, clapping her hands. "Let's hoop. None of us know what's gonna happen next year, so right now we gotta focus on this year. This year we are *going* to win the Invitational, but that means that we gotta get serious. Now."

Who knows if Tamika's pep talk actually works, or if the guys are just willing to fake it till they make it, but one by one they each grab a ball and spread out on the court. Chris is the last to join the group, and just before he does, Dex pulls him aside.

"I'm really sorry about the thing with you and Kendrick," he says, "but I was thinking it might be good for you to write about it. You know, for your Creative Writing assignment."

"Yeeeah, I don't know if I really wanna do that, though. It's just . . . a lot right now. With my dad and everything, I just . . . I don't know."

"Oh, yeah, right," Dex says, waving his hand. "I totally get that. Definitely don't write about it if it's still too weird."

"Yeah," Chris says. "It's definitely still weird."

"Well," Dex adds, his face warm with embarrassment,

"I meant what I said about helping you out with your assignment. If you need anything, just let me know."

Chris smiles. "Thanks, but I think I got it. You said you'd help me to try to get me to join Hoop Group, but you don't have to worry about that now. Now I'm here 'cause I really wanna be here."

CHAPTER 24

AFTER HOOP GROUP PRACTICE, Tamika is back at home and practicing her fadeaway, jacking up shot after shot as she wrestles with problems too big for her twelve-year-old mind to solve. Tamika was able to put on a good face for the remainder of Hoop Group practice, but now, in the comfort of her driveway, she lets all the emotion that she'd pushed down bubble freely to the surface of her soul.

An hour later, when her arms hang soft like Jell-O and she's all cried out, Tamika walks back into the house for dinner. Her father is standing at the kitchen counter by then, his lips betraying a rare moment of joy. "I was watching you out there," he says. "You look good. Strong. Y'all might actually do something in the tourney this weekend."

Tamika studies her father's face, searching for sincerity. She is skeptical, but she responds anyway: "Yeah, Dad. We *are* gonna do something. We're gonna win."

Coach Beck shrugs. "Maybe so. I see Jayden—"

Tamika cuts her father off mid-sentence. "We were good before Jayden came back to the team, you know."

"Okay, fine." Coach Beck raises his hands in surrender. "You big-time now. Got it. So tell me, then: If you're so sure y'all are gonna win, what are you so mad about? You only shoot like that when something's bothering you."

Against her better judgment, Tamika tells her father about Principal Kim's announcement and how, when Dex suggested that Chris ask Kendrick King to help, Chris admitted that he hadn't spoken to his uncle in a long time. She also tells her father that, while she wants to win on Saturday, she's even more worried about next year.

"Maybe . . . ," Tamika starts slowly, "if you can't help us keep the program together . . . maybe . . . you could . . . um . . . reach out to Kendrick yourself?"

Coach Beck's laugh is so loud and so gaudy—obnoxious

like a hot-pink dress with rhinestones *and* sequins—that it catches Tamika by complete surprise.

"Next year?" Coach Beck says, his laughter starting to taper. "There is no next year—not with basketball, not for you. It's time for you to get realistic about your future and start focusing on other things."

Again, Tamika's heart drops at her father's contempt. But this time, she doesn't second-guess the voice in her head or stop herself from saying what she feels.

"I'm so sorry that I'm not a boy like Jayden," she says. "I'm so sorry that it embarrasses you that your daughter wants to play in the WNBA. I'm sorry that you don't love me enough to support what *I* want to do. But I'm done trying. And as soon as Mom tells me it's okay for me to go back to Austinberg, I'm out of here."

Tamika isn't expecting the sadness in her father's eyes or the slouch of his shoulders, but seeing them brings the first bit of satisfaction she's felt in his presence in some time.

As she spins on her heels to run away, Tamika easily shakes free of her father's hand grasping for her arm. The swift motion sends his body tumbling backward, his arms flailing wildly, and this brings vindication, too.

Tamika is surprised by her strength, by her ability to prove her father wrong. But as she turns down the hallway on the way to her room—the sanctuary gilded with posters of Candace Parker, Aari McDonald, and Sabrina Ionescu—something else surprises her.

It is a sound, a sickening thud to be exact, and it follows her from the kitchen. As soon as Tamika hears it, she turns and finds her father, the great Coach Beck, lying motionless on the floor.

CHAPTER 25

H E'S BEEN WORKING ON IT for weeks, but after too many revisions to count, Anthony is finally proud of his work, a collection of poems capped off with a piece he wrote specifically for Tamika.

Anthony knows how nervous Tamika is about the tournament—no matter how confident she tries to appear—and he hopes his words will help put her at ease. It's taken him two whole weeks to get past his own anxiety about sharing the poem with her, but now that they're just one day away from the final game of the Fall Invitational, he knows he can't wait any longer.

He'd planned to slip it to her before practice starts,

maybe slide it in her backpack when she wasn't looking, but when Anthony arrives at the gym, he is surprised to find that Dex is the only other Hoop Grouper present. Tamika is nowhere around, and he immediately senses that something is wrong. Since the beginning of the year, Anthony has always been one of the last to arrive. Things have changed a bit, and he definitely likes the game a lot more than he did a couple of months ago, but he's still not eager enough to beat Tamika to the gym.

During Creative Writing class, Jayden said that he'd be a little late to practice, and Chris noted that he probably wouldn't make it at all, thanks to an already rescheduled dentist appointment. But no one had heard from Tamika, and it wasn't like her to not be on time.

Thirty minutes later, Anthony's worry has reached its peak when Principal Kim walks in, her eyes glistening and lips trembling. "Tamika won't be at practice today," she says. "Coach Beck had a pretty bad fall yesterday evening. He hit his head and is in surgery now. They're not sure . . . They're not sure he's going to make it."

Anthony doesn't have time to process all of Principal Kim's words. All he knows is that he needs to get to Tamika. "Where is she?" he asks.

"Lorain Medical Center," Principal Kim says through tears. "With her mother."

Tamika is pacing. Back and forth, back and forth, she walks across the nearly empty waiting area. The only other person in the room is her mother, and she is the one who greets Anthony and Dex when they arrive. After a grief-filled greeting, Tamika's mom explains what her daughter is too devastated to say herself:

When Coach Beck reached out for Tamika's arm, he lost his balance. As he was falling, he hit the right side of his head on the corner of the kitchen counter. He was lucky that Tamika was there when it happened and was able to call an ambulance quickly—any longer and he may not have survived. Unfortunately, since arriving at the hospital, Coach Beck has also suffered multiple seizures.

Doctors aren't sure if his seizures were triggered by the injury, which is entirely possible, or if they are a result of his progressing Parkinson's disease. The doctors put him in a medically induced coma to avoid further damage to his brain. The good news is that he has been under for almost eighteen hours, and doctors agree that things are improving.

When Tamika's mother finishes, Anthony and Dex

shift their eyes to Tamika, who is still walking the length of the room.

"I'm so sorry, Tamika," Dex says. "I can't imagine—"

In a rush, Tamika turns to Dex, her cheeks wet and blotchy, her eyes dim. "Why are you here? You guys should have stayed and practiced without me."

"We wanted to see how you were doing," Anthony says. "Plus, it wouldn't have felt right to practice without you."

Tamika finally collapses into one of the plastic blue chairs. "Well, that's what you're gonna have to do from now on, so you might as well get used to it. I'm done with basketball."

"Tamika, baby, you don't mean that," her mother says from across the room.

"Actually, I do. Dad was right. It's time for me to grow up."

Tamika pauses, takes a deep breath, and smooths the wrinkled Cleveland Rockers T-shirt she's been wearing since Hoop Group practice the day before. "I need to start thinking about my future." Turning to Dex and Anthony, she adds, "It's been great playing with you guys, and I wish y'all the best tomorrow. But I'm quitting Hoop Group."

Dex wants to respond, but he knows it's no use. Especially when Anthony says that if Tamika's quitting, he is, too.

For days, the Fall Invitational has been all Jayden can think about, especially after learning that Hoop Group would be facing off against Marcus Cheney and the Avon Lake Rebels in the championship. If Marcus is half the competitor Jayden thinks he is, he's going to be seeking retribution for his loss in the vertical leap-off at the Shoot, Dunk, and Spin Classic. These were the thoughts crowding his mind when he walked to Slice after school to pick up his paycheck.

Don't worry about it, Roddy told Jayden when he saw the worried look on his face. *As long as you play your game and keep driving no matter what, you got this.*

Roddy's words were enough to calm Jayden's concerns, at least for the moment. And as he left Slice to head back to Carter Middle, the blue of the sky was especially bright, the crisp October wind whipping around his bare legs so energizing that he decided to run the rest of the way.

He was excited about practice, ready for one final

run-through with his team before tomorrow's big show. But now that he's back in the Carter Middle School gym, Jayden is alone. There is no sign of Anthony, Dex, or Chris. The biggest surprise is that Tamika isn't there, either.

Jayden assumes that maybe they finished practicing early, that perhaps Tamika suggested they get home so they can rest up. For a second, he considers going home, too.

But he doesn't. Instead, Jayden grabs a ball and starts hooping. He moves through the same drills that he did in the early morning on the first day of Hoop Group. His steps are quicker, though; his shot is sharper; and his body slides across the floor with the confidence of a kid who is less than twenty-four hours from seeing his dreams come true.

CHAPTER 26

THE NEXT MORNING, Jayden is up by 7:00. It's still hours before Hoop Group's game is scheduled to start, but late enough that Jayden can't even think about going back to sleep. His nerves are crackling; his shooting hand's itching; and with visions of the Fall Invitational trophy dancing in his head, he coaxes his mother and Grams out of their sleep. He wants to get to the courts as soon as possible.

When he arrives, Jayden watches a finals matchup from another age group and does some light jogging to loosen up. Later, about ninety minutes before his team is supposed to check in with the officials, Jayden gets in his first shots of the day, lets the clap of the ball against the backboard soothe him. He isn't warming up long when he sees coaches from some of the area prep schools take seats around the court, including Coach McGrath from Willow Brook Academy.

Camera crews from the local news stations are setting up, too, and now Jayden can feel the electricity in the air, the intensity of the upcoming competition. It's really real, and every move Jayden makes from that moment on must be intentional, precise.

Jayden is visualizing plays in his mind, seeing himself strike early and often, from in- and outside the paint. He is ready; he knows he is. And he can't wait for the game to begin so he can show Coach McGrath and all the others that he's as good as any kid who ever came out of Lorain.

But there's just one problem: Jayden has no idea where the rest of his team is.

It was after 11:00 on Friday night when Coach Beck's doctors made one last evaluation of his progress and decided that he had, in fact, improved enough to be taken out of his medically induced coma. It was the first positive sign since he'd collapsed, and it was enough of a sign for Tamika to finally close her eyes and catch a few moments of sleep.

The next morning when Coach Beck's doctor gently shook her awake, she was groggy, her brain foggy. She couldn't remember why she'd slept in a hospital waiting room chair, had forgotten all about her father's long, long night. But the doctor told her that Coach Beck had finally turned the corner. They'd just turned off the propofol drip in his IV, and now he was awake and asking for his daughter.

Tamika walks into her father's room alone, and seeing him so weak, so fragile, causes her to burst into tears immediately.

"I'm so sorry, Dad," she cries. "About everything. I've been thinking about it, and I understand. I really do."

Coach Beck shakes his head and tries to stop her, but he can't. Tamika has been practicing for this moment ever since the paramedics lifted his limp body off their kitchen floor.

"I don't care about any of it anymore," she adds. "If

you don't want me to play basketball, I won't. I just want you to be happy—and alive . . ."

Tamika is still rambling, water falling from her eyes and onto her father's frail hand that she is clutching so tightly.

"Tamika, honey," Coach Beck says, his voice barely above a whisper. "I need to tell you something."

He stops to take a sip of water from the pitcher on the table next to him. "This may sound strange, but when I was still in the coma, I felt the presence of the Lord like I never have before."

Coach Beck pauses again, this time to wipe away the tears that are starting to tumble down his own cheeks. "God didn't speak audibly, but He told me, in a way that's far more meaningful than words, that I need to learn to love you better."

With a deep sigh, he adds, "You love basketball, don't you?"

Tamika hesitates only briefly before nodding. "Yeah, Dad. I do."

"I know you do, baby. And I'm sorry for making you feel bad about that. I was just trying to do right by you. You're my *child*, and I've always felt it was my job to protect you. But that doesn't give me a right to keep you from what you love."

Tamika is stunned and silent, and the tears just keep flowing.

"We don't get to decide who we are, just like we don't get to decide who or what we love. You are a basketball player, Tamika. You're an *incredible* basketball player, actually, and I want you to go as far as you want to go in this sport. We only get so much time on this Earth, and I'm going to spend the rest of my life helping you toward your dreams, if you'll let me."

Tamika throws herself onto the bed and wraps her arms around her father. "Thank you, Daddy. Thank you for saying all of that."

"Sure thing," Coach Beck says, looking at the clock. "Now, don't you think it's time for you to get going? You're the captain, right? I'm sure your team needs you."

Tamika doesn't want to leave, but Coach Beck assures her that he'll be there when she gets back. Then, just before she walks out the door, he tells her to win for him and for the city of Lorain. But most of all, he tells her to win for herself.

"I don't know what's going to happen," he adds, "but

if this whole experience has taught me anything, it's that the good Lord always has a plan."

Within moments, Tamika is on the phone with Dex and Anthony, telling them that she's back in Hoop Group and ready to destroy the Rebels. An hour later, the three of them are walking onto the tournament's main court, where Jayden is currently practicing free throws.

Jayden is thrilled to see them finally arrive, but he is just as surprised as they are to see that Chris hasn't arrived. The Rebels, meanwhile, are fourteen-deep, running layup lines on the opposite goal. There's not much time left before the game is set to begin, and the Hoop Groupers are starting to worry.

Without Chris, they're right back to where they started. They won't have enough players, and they'll surely have to forfeit.

CHAPTER 27

IT IS DÉJÀ VU, this feeling of defeat that nearly suf-focates Tamika as she begins a slow stroll to the judges' table. It's the same walk she'd made weeks prior, during the Shoot, Dunk, and Spin Classic, when she was cer-tain that the four-man Hoop Group wouldn't be able to participate in the fifth and final competition. Jayden saved them that day, but she can't imagine that they will be that lucky again. So she pastes on a smile, one that starts out phony but grows increasingly genuine as she thinks back to the events of that morning. The day before, she wasn't sure if her father was going to survive through the night. What right does she have to be upset about a silly basketball game?

Then she remembers her father's words: *The good Lord always has a plan.*

If she's being honest, Tamika isn't sure she believes that, but maybe . . .

Suddenly, Tamika's thoughts are interrupted by a commotion, some cheers and applause that start farther down the shore but grow closer and closer until they arrive at the same court where Hoop Group is set to tip off. Tamika turns and sees Chris strolling, grinning. He stops where Anthony, Dex, and Jayden are gathered, and Tamika makes her way over, too. Of course, Chris's presence is enough to lift her sprits—now Hoop Group has enough players to compete—but she realizes that he's not the reason the crowd is roaring.

That distinction belongs to Kendrick King, who just stepped onto the court.

As Kendrick introduces himself to the team, Jayden manages to maintain his composure. Dex, however, is not so reserved. His voice rises a whole octave, and he's talking so fast that his words trip over each other as he counts down his favorite Kendrick King plays of all time: there's the dunk over Billy Malone in last year's Slam Dunk challenge, the buzzer beater that clinched his team's playoff spot the season before that, the—

Kendrick chuckles and puts an arm around Dex's shoulders. "We have time to talk about all that later, trust me," he tells Dex. "Right now, all I wanna talk about is Hoop Group."

"Did you come to watch us play?" Dex says, still amazed.

"I'm definitely gonna watch," Kendrick says, "but I actually came to see if I could help out. Maybe coach y'all a little bit."

"Are you *serious*?" Tamika says. "That's amazing! But I don't understand. How did you know—"

Now Kendrick throws his arm around Chris, who's still standing next to him, still cheesing from ear to ear. "My nephew sent me an email and told me about y'all's season. Said y'all could use a little help."

Tamika's eyes grow wide like basketball rims. "So you're going to save the program?"

"Once a Hoop Grouper, always a Hoop Grouper," Kendrick says. "But before we get to talking about the program, I think there's some business we need to attend to first. Right now, we need to show the Rebels how we do it."

With Kendrick coaching on the sidelines, Hoop Group plays an incredible game that is tight from the very beginning. The Rebels are efficient and well trained, and they have enough players to always keep fresh legs on the floor. But what Hoop Group lacks in skills and manpower, they more than make up for with enthusiasm and hunger.

And they have Jayden.

No one ever doubted Jayden's ability, but this game has brought the best out of him. He's been matched up against Marcus Cheney the whole afternoon, and he's refused to back down, swarming him on D and keeping him guessing on offense.

Going into the fourth quarter, the game is tied, and the crowd gathered around the court has tripled in size. Many are there to see Kendrick, of course, but others seem to know that this is the only game that matters, that this is the game that will determine Lorain's youth basketball bragging rights for years to come.

There are only twenty seconds left in the game, and Hoop Group is down by four when Tamika gets fouled and sent to the line. The pressure is crazy, and her ankle is throbbing after a rough fall, but Tamika is the epitome of grace under fire. She sinks both free throws, leaving Hoop Group down by two with only one remaining time out.

The Rebels have possession, and if they are smart with the ball, they will simply hold it and run the clock down to zero. All it would take is a quick game of keep-away to snuff out any chance of a Hoop Group victory.

Luckily, before Hoop Group is counted out for good, Dex is able to steal the ball back. And with twelve seconds on the clock, he calls for a time out.

There's time for just one more shot.

Hoop Group gathers on the sideline. Tamika can barely move, but with only five players on the squad, Kendrick can't pull her out. Ideally, he'd draw up a fake that pulls the defense to her side so she can kick it back to Jayden, but he knows that Jayden, who's the leading scorer on both teams, will be double-teamed. He decides, instead, to run the play for Chris.

A couple of months ago, this decision would have caused a war in Chris's heart. While he would have been afraid to take the shot, he would have demanded it. But so much has changed since then. Now the decision is easy.

"Give it to Jayden," Chris says. "He's hot, and this is his game."

Kendrick locks eyes with Chris for a long moment before turning back to Jayden. "They're gonna be all over you," Kendrick says. "You sure you can make the shot?"

"Absolutely," Jayden says without hesitation. "Get it to me, and I'll drain it."

After an in-bounds from Anthony and a backbreaking pick by Dex, the ball lands in Jayden's hands at the corner. And all at once, like it always does, the world around him collapses. The crowd goes mute and everything begins moving in slow motion.

Jayden watches Marcus, crouched low, and takes a quick step to his right. It's a test, and when Marcus shifts out of position ever so slightly, Jayden sees his internal dialogue, how he beats himself up for falling for the fake. Jayden then smiles to himself, knowing he has Marcus right where he wants him.

The next step—this time to his left—is even quicker, stronger, and Marcus dives wildly, tumbling onto the concrete. With nothing but space and opportunity,

Jayden steps behind the three-point line, sets himself, and launches from deep.

Seconds later, the crowd breaks into applause again, but it's not for Kendrick King. This time, it's for Jayden Carr. His three-pointer was all net, and Hoop Group has won the game!

CHAPTER 28

THE BASKETBALL COURT has erupted into absolute mayhem as the crowd swarms Hoop Group and its new superstar coach. At the same time, Coach Beck is watching it all from his hospital bed, his heart bursting with pride for his team and, most of all, his daughter. He is still watching as Anthony slips what looks like a square of folded paper into Tamika's pocket just before a commentator from WXKZ News 9 steps into the frame.

"Congratulations on an incredible win, Mr. King," says the bubbly brunette who's holding a microphone up to Kendrick's mouth. "It seems like such a bittersweet ending to such a storied program in our city, though. Can you comment on reports that this will be Hoop Group's last year?"

Kendrick grabs the mic and says, emphatically, "Hoop Group is definitely *not* over! I grew up in this program. It's a safe space to learn a great game, and as long as there are kids who want to participate, I want to make sure Hoop Group continues." He stops for a moment and turns to face the camera directly. "Coach Beck, I know you weren't able to be here today, but I hope we made you proud. We did this for you!"

Coach Beck is wiping away tears as the reporter heads over to speak to the Rebels coach. "You know Kendrick King?" asks the nurse who just came in to give him his afternoon meds.

"Sure do. Used to coach him when he was a kid."

Now the nurse is stunned silent, seemingly forgetting about the paper cup in her hand that cradles Coach Beck's meds. "Wow. That's so cool to have coached a big star like Kendrick."

Coach lifts the cup out of the nurse's hand and, with a quick sip of water, swallows all the pills at once. "No," he says a moment later. "The real star is my daughter. She's the reason they won today."

Now that the rush of the game has passed, Jayden has a moment to reflect on the wildest, most exhilarating afternoon of his life. He hit a game-winning shot for Hoop Group, *and* he was coached by his all-time favorite basketball player.

"You did your thing out there," Kendrick tells him as he daps him up. "I'm proud of you, for real."

Jayden shakes his head in disbelief. "Thanks, Coach Kendrick. I'm just glad you came. Hoop Group is everything to me, and we wouldn't even be here if it wasn't for you."

"It's all good, Jayden. You don't need to thank me. And as a matter of fact, I wanted to get with you about something else. I've been thinking about funding a handful of new after-school programs in the community—maybe expanding Hoop Group to other schools—but I'mma definitely need help running them." He smiles and motions to the corner of the court where Jayden's mom and Grams are standing. "I hear your mom is great at making a little go a long way. . . . You think she'd be up for the job?"

There's no way Jayden heard that right. "You wanna

hire . . . my mom?" he says.

Kendrick laughs. "Yeah, man. I mean, if she wants to work with me."

"Of course she does! I mean, I'm sure she'd say yes if you asked her. In fact, I'll go ask her now!"

Jayden takes off running and races right past Tamika, who's standing on the edge of the crowd. While reaching into her pocket for a piece of gum, she finds the paper that Anthony placed there. As she unfolds the paper and begins to read, she notices Anthony's handwriting.

Tamika:

I've tried to find the words to say

What you've meant this year

But every time I search my heart

My nervousness remains

I may not write so well, it's true

But what I'll say is this

In a world of wind and storms above

You're a shelter from the rain

Tamika carefully refolds the poem and returns it to her pocket. She is flattered and grateful. In her mind, Hoop Group was all about basketball and carving out her own legacy apart from her famous father. She never imagined that the team would provide the friendships she needed most.

Tamika runs over to Anthony and wraps her arms around him in a big, sweaty embrace. The words are unspoken, but they're there, the mutual appreciation and respect between good friends.

Meanwhile, with the crowds thinning and the news crews departed, Kendrick turns his attention to his nephew.

"I'm glad you reached out," Kendrick tells him, "but it didn't have to be about basketball. You know that, right?"

Chris shrugs.

"And you know that whatever is going on between me and your dad is between me and your dad, right?"

Another shrug.

Kendrick sighs, then takes another approach. "I'm sorry, Chris. Okay? I'm not gonna speak for your dad, but if you felt like you couldn't talk to me because of whatever me and him are dealing with, that's my fault. It's grown folks' business and it ain't got nothing to do with me and you. I'mma do a better job of letting you know that. Okay?"

Now Chris nods and nods and wraps his arms tight around Kendrick's waist. "I love you, Uncle Ken," he says.

"I love you, too, Chris."

Jayden breaks through the crowd and finally finds his mom, standing with her back to him, her hands waving widely. As he approaches, Jayden is already talking, sharing the good news from Kendrick: "Mom!" he yells. "Kendrick King is gonna save Hoop Group! And start a bunch of other after-school programs! And he wants you to run them! Like, you'd get to work for *Kendrick King*! How cool is that!"

Jayden's mom turns around with a smile, and as soon as she does, Jayden can finally see the person standing just past her. It's Coach McGrath from Willow Brook.

"Jayden," his mom says, "I want to introduce you to Coach Justin McGrath. He was really impressed by your playing today, and he wants to talk to you about joining his team next year."

In an instant, Jayden is speechless. It's all he's ever hoped for, all of it, in this moment.

"That's right," Coach McGrath says, shaking Jayden's hand. "Our starting two guard from last year is moving to Chicago with his family, so we have an empty roster spot that we think is just your size." He pauses and looks to Jayden's mom, then back to Jayden.

Jayden smiles, nods, and says, "Yes, sir, thank you SO much for the opportunity," but he's not sure how he even formed a complete sentence. His head is a tangle of thoughts. He wants to play at Willow Brook, the prep school that developed his idol, Kendrick King. . . .

But what about Hoop Group?

"When do you guys practice?" Jayden says, already crunching his calendar in his mind. "Hoop Group practices are three to five, so if I'm going to play for Hoop Group and Willow Brook—"

"Oh, no, Jayden," Coach McGrath says, interrupting. "I'm sorry, but you wouldn't be able to play for Willow Brook and Hoop Group at the same time. There's just too much of a commitment required at this level. Now, we definitely think we have a lot to offer a talented young player like you, but you will have to make that choice."

Jayden looks to his mother, but her face is blank, a signal that he will have to make this decision completely on his own. He has no idea how he'll do it, but on this day, with the sun high and shining, he doesn't even want to think about it. Right now, all he wants to think about is his win, his mom's new job, and the power of *hope*.

Coach McGrath shakes Jayden's hand one final time while saying that he'll be in touch. Moments later, just as he is walking away, Jayden is swarmed by his teammates. They circle him in a giant group hug while shouting *"Hoop Group forever! Hoop Group forever!"*

Their collective voices are just loud enough to rise above the din, and while Jayden doesn't know if he will actually stay with Hoop Group forever, he's happy to get caught up in the emotion of the moment. Right now it feels nice to not have to think about anything else besides hanging with his new best friends, his new family.